Dear Keith,

Please enjoy,

Maurice

Darlo Reprised

By

Maurice Horner

About The Author

Maurice Horner was pleased to have been born in Darlington which, for him, was one of the finest towns in County Durham. It was a town that didn't try to capture him but allowed him to flourish, it armed him with the tools he needed to venture into the world.

He ended up in New Zealand where he has lived for more years than anywhere else including the country of his birth.

Notwithstanding, his North of England accent is still recognisable, albeit somewhat more muted these days and generously spiced with New Zealand idioms.

Anyone wishing to contact the author may do so at
rtntodarlo@outlook.co.nz

Darlo Reprised

First Printing, 2022

ISBN: 9780473652500

Acknowledgements

Thanks to my daughter Elspeth and son Jonathan for all
their considerable help and encouragement in
writing the Darlo Trilogy.

A special big thank you to my wife Jenny who has helped so
much that she should really be a joint author.

Thanks to Jim Olson for giving me one of his tales to tell,
and...
thanks to Jenny Harrison and the nurses of Darlington Memorial Hospital
for their memories and assistance.

Other Books in the Series

Tales of Darlo

Return to Darlo

Available through Amazon.

Contents

Introduction 11
The Priest's Story 17
What Goes Around 25
The Good Luck Charm 31
Be Careful What You Chew On 41
Patience Is Rewarded 49
I Cannot Tell a Lie 59
The War Ace 67
Family Secrets 71
Ghost Story 81
Web of Deceit 89
Business As Unusual 109
Love and War 117
The Dilemma 129

Introduction

It was a long time since Dave had last stood beneath the Town Clock Tower, a sombre piece of Victorian Gothic brick and stone that looked down upon its denizens. People used to scurry around in its shadow to change buses and dash into and out of the covered market. They hastened over the pedestrian crossing that periodically halted the constant flow of traffic on the main road between London and Edinburgh. It was the centre for the Grammar School boys to congregate before they headed up Post House Wynd and Duke Street on their way to school. It was as busy as the entrance of a beehive on a sunny summer's day when many flowers are in bloom.

People came, met, chatted, rattled their dags, as you'd say in New Zealand, and moved on only to be replaced by others doing the same thing. There used to be a constant vitality which Dave was no longer noticing. There were people about but not crowds, they were ambling more than dashing. The 'for sale' and 'to let signs' in Post House Wynd seemed to suggest a tiredness, a resignation, a forlornness. Where were the outdoor market traders plying their wares sheltering under the market's canopy brightened up by Charlie Hall's wonderful display on his flower stall? Dave wondered if the new ski ramp to the side door of the market hosted political rallies just as the old stone steps used to. The speeches, the hecklers, the opponents trying to grab handfuls of the pamphlets to run away with them. It was all serious fun.

Dave wondered if he was being over critical. Was he being as arrogant as some of the visiting overseas managers that he'd heard about in New Zealand? Their visits became known as 'management by seagull'. They would fly in, squawk and flap about a lot, consume copious amounts of food and wine at the finest restaurants available and take off again before dropping their guano from a great height over those they had visited. All of this would be stoically accepted by the locals knowing that once they'd gone they could get on and do what they did well until another interruption in a couple of years' time. There were exceptions when the degree of arrogance punctured the benign balloon and the game of due deference gave way to reveal that streak that has made the All Blacks what they can be.

Such was the case of a German visiting in the 1960s. He was being shown around branches throughout New Zealand as well as being given a sightseeing tour. Nothing could make this man happy. Everything was bigger, brighter and better in Germany from the widgets produced to the Southern Alps, from paperwork to pristine beaches. He seemed unable to make any comment other than a disparaging one. As he was being driven to his next location and knowing Kiwis are well travelled, he asked the driver if he had ever been to Germany. The driver said he had.

"And which part of Germany did you like the best?" enquired the visitor. The driver paused for a moment,

"The orange glow in the sky" he replied, "when the bomber turned for home." The rest of the journey was conducted in silence.

Dave's friend in Richmond had said Darlington was still a great town and that you could get almost everything you wanted there and who was Dave to disagree. Certainly, a far cry from his early days in New Zealand, where it wasn't unusual to be told when shopping that they were waiting for a ship to arrive. Equally it wasn't uncommon to be directed to another shop who might have what you wanted or were selling the goods more cheaply. The friendly Kiwi trait was endearing even if it did rapidly disappear once they were behind the steering wheel of a car.

Dave reflected that he'd lived for more years in New Zealand than he had in the UK. Although, if he and his wife had been given an easy option to return in the first couple of weeks after arriving in New Zealand they'd probably have taken it.

Dave and his wife's journey had begun in an old DC3 aeroplane flying from Middleton St George, Teesside, to Heathrow. Amidst tears and excitement the plane stood at the end of the runway with its brakes on, the pilot wound up the engines, the propellers became more and more of a blur, the noise increased, the plane vibrated like crazy and then the pilot took the brakes off and down the runway they went. It was Dave's first flight. Apparently, this particular plane had had a history of blowing its air seals around the door, the bang was dramatic for the passengers but not the staff who were used to it. With the rapid decompression the plane then had to drop down and fly at a much lower altitude. Thankfully, Dave and his wife were spared this drama but not his friend John in later months.

From Heathrow they flew on an Air New Zealand DC10 plane to Auckland arriving one day late as Los Angeles was fog bound. They were diverted to Las Vegas to stay overnight. Some bureaucratic juggling was needed as Dave and his wife, along with a few others, didn't have a US visa. Passports were confiscated only to be handed back on their departure, along with those for some of the other passengers. The overnight stop in a beautiful hotel room with some of the softest pillows in the world was magic and set a principle to try to follow on future long haul flights.

Guy Fawkes would have been delighted to hear that this was the year when Dave and his wife lost November the 5th due to the vagaries of the international date line.

The flight from Las Vegas to Los Angeles and on to Auckland via Rarotonga was uneventful but the terminal at Auckland airport came as a surprise. It was a far cry from the professional hunk of concrete hosting a myriad of duty free shops and cafes that visitors experience in the 21st century. Its architectural inspiration was a cross between an agricultural corrugated iron barn and a sheep shearing shed.

There was more than one thing that seemed set to discourage them in their first couple of weeks in New Zealand. The person who was meant to meet them at the airport was late and they had no idea where their accommodation was. Cars were relatively expensive in New Zealand and it would have been advantageous to ship their car but were told there no Simcas 'down under'. Almost the first car they pulled up behind on their way from the airport was a Simca.

In the first couple of days they went out and bought a car, a Vauxhall Viva, and a week later crashed it. They'd come to a three way junction and were uncertain as to who had the right of way given the anachronistic rules of the road that existed in New Zealand at the time. It was no consolation that years later the weird 'give way to vehicles on the right' rule was changed. At the time, all seemed clear when they were helpfully waved across by a man in a large American style car. Dave ventured forth only to be met by a pre-war car with inadequate brakes coming from the other arm of the junction. That car bounced off Dave's Viva into the helpful man's car who, on closer encounter with his breath, had obviously been paying his respects at the Temple of Bacchus.

The consequent meeting with the insurance company also had its moments. Dave found Kiwis pronounced vowels in a way his ear had not yet adjusted to. There were some definite differences in the use of English, but not quite as bad as those between Newcastle and Essex, for example. Notwithstanding, the differences were bad enough. Dave was wondering why the person dealing with his insurance claim kept asking him if he had a pin. He was baffled as to why they would think he would have a pin on him. The light dawned when a biro was waved at him and yes he did have a pen.

Dave and his wife had opened up a New Zealand bank account whilst in Britain and had been assured that, having done that, they would be guaranteed a mortgage when they arrived in New Zealand. When they visited the bank in Auckland to enquire about their mortgage they were met with a merriment almost verging on the hysteria. Dave and his wife wondered what on earth had they done. If they could have turned the clock back a couple of weeks they surely would have.

Then, bit by bit, things started to improve and they adapted quickly to their new lives. They made sure they were more familiar with the rules of the road and quickly passed their local driving test. They became used to late night shopping knowing that in those days, all shops were closed at the weekend. They quickly settled into their new jobs. Dave's wife, having been a health visitor in the U.K. joined the Plunket Society which looked after the health of children up to 5 years old. She worked in an area with a large community from the Pacific Islands so had to quickly learn about and be sensitive to their cultures and where necessary gently guide them through some of their naivety. For instance, a family had heard a name they really liked the sound of and wanted to call their child that. Dave's wife gently suggested alternative names that would better for their child rather than their proposal of Gonorrhoea.

Dave and his wife's first Christmas was going to be spent at the beach. The picnic was packed and they were ready to go when friends turned up at the door, they wouldn't take 'no' for an answer and whisked them away to spend Christmas at a family member's vineyard.

Maybe New Zealand was going to work out for them after all.

Chapter One
The Priest's Story

Dave left the shadow of the Clock Tower and walked over the pedestrian precinct occupying what used to be the main and very busy road between London and Scotland. He avoided the Dalek ramps and walked up the steps on to the High Row near where Martin's Bank used to be. He looked back along Tubwell Row. Dave thought it must have been round about that spot where Lindsay Bird had made a sketch for one of his paintings that showed an endless parade of floats coming along West Row. He wondered if there was anywhere in Britain that still had parades like that these days that resembled the

Christmas parades he used to attend with his children in New Zealand. As he looked down Tubwell Row Dave noticed the spire of St Cuthbert's Church. It was a lovely 12/13th century church vandalised by the Victorians.

Dave recalled that in his younger days Peter Wansey had been the man in charge. Had he been the Dean of Darlington? Maybe so, he couldn't fully recall. He'd certainly been a big gun in the church. 'Come to think of it,' Dave thought, 'that had to be true, after all he was a Canon.' Dave had a little chuckle to himself. He recalled that Peter said he had a friend whose daughter had a teddy bear called Gladly. It had been much loved and hugged to the extent that its head had become squashed and distorted such that its eyes displayed a distinct squint. Peter teased the girl by telling her that his favourite hymn was 'Gladly, the cross eyed bear.' Over the years Dave had heard the same story more than once and in different contexts and had even seen a book with that title but Peter's version was the first time he'd ever heard it.

Now that Dave's mind was on the subject of men of the cloth he recalled one who stood out, amongst those he had encountered in days gone by, called Danny. When Dave first knew him, he was on the flamboyant side of life. He cut a dapper figure with a liking for brightly coloured waistcoats, Harris Tweed jackets and highly polished knee-high boots. His parishioners thought the world of him and he threw himself into any and every good deed going. He was affable, easy going and smiled a lot. Even if you didn't agree with him people felt guilty about disagreeing with him. He was happily married with a pigeon pair, a boy and a girl. His children were a little less reverential to him and at times treated him as if he was the worst and unwanted middle-aged dancer at a children's birthday party. They thought it would be nice, at times, if the family was a little less in the limelight.

Danny had a degree in a subject of no great consequence from a red brick university. The rumour machine had it that whilst studying Danny had taken up with a girl who subsequently became pregnant. Sadly, the relationship broke down. For reasons that Dave could not quite comprehend this had resulted in Danny finding God and attending Theological College. Danny's God seemed a very practical and down to earth God that his parishioners could relate to. His theosophy wasn't couched in the archaic linguistics of the Bible. He spoke simply about his beliefs and in the language of the day. The only trouble he suffered from was that it seemed all and sundry wanted a part of him. He rationed his time well enough that no one felt neglected or aggrieved. His Bishop was pleased with both the size of his congregation as well as the size of the collection plate. He was destined for greater things within the Church and had made more than one friend in the Bishop's Palace.

All looked well, in fact better than well, so when it happened no one was prepared or expected it, including his family. The job meant that you couldn't escape deaths. It came with the territory. Danny had built up his coping mechanisms but more than that his sympathy and empathy with his parishioners had given comfort to many a grieving family. He could see that he did make a difference for the better and had brought the comfort of God to the people in need. His funeral services recognised the sadness but also encouraged the joy, the celebration of a life that had been and, not to be underrated, the wake. In his time he'd buried those hardly born through to nonagenarians, each had its challenges but each seemed to end with a peace and calmness as the departed souls were committed to God's care.

So why was this one different? Danny couldn't tell you. Even many years after the event he still couldn't talk about it.

An eight year old boy, an only child, who had been taken ill and died in short order. The funeral service was sombre, even by funeral service standards. In the course of it, Danny had raised the question of where was God? Uncharacteristically, he didn't even try to answer the question.

Shortly after, Danny took to kneeling before the altar for hours on end which then turned into all night vigils. He didn't want to talk to his wife and started to ignore his children. He became unkempt, unshaven and un-showered. He didn't change his clothes and ate very little. It wasn't only his personal hygiene that he neglected, also he neglected his parochial duties.

His wife sought help but had difficulty getting people to understand. The Church quickly wanted to get him away from his Parish so that he wasn't seen as a scandal but assessed that he was only a little tired given everything in which he was involved. They thought a couple of weeks holiday at Scarborough would see him right.

His wife knew otherwise and knew he needed psychiatric aid but she couldn't find anyone to give him the help that he required. She could see things were getting worse and she became concerned about her safety. He started to become very angry with her for no apparent reason and accused her of being in league with the Devil. He would order her out of his sight. He then turned on his children shouting at them that they were the Devil incarnate and they should burn in Hell. They were dismayed and frightened. One afternoon, after a harangue that left his wife and children both frightened and in tears she felt she had no choice. She left with her children and headed for her parent's home.

When she was safely away she telephoned the Bishop's office to let them know what the situation was. They immediately sent someone to catch up with Danny and see if, with the help of some appropriate counselling, they couldn't get him on the straight and narrow again. Danny was found in the church praying. Gentle persuasion and back rubbing had no effect on Danny's desire to prostrate himself before God. When a firmer hand was used to try and remove him from the Church he became angry and grabbed the crucifix from the altar and started swinging it about. He caught the would be counsellor above the eye and drew blood. Fortunately, now he could be sectioned under the Mental Health Act and receive the help that his wife knew that he needed.

The hospital Danny was sent to was on the edge of a village in the countryside. His first days and weeks were a haze to him. It was a regime of locked wards and padded cells. He was given drugs and electrotherapy, he hated that as it not only disorientated him but he felt it disabled him, his brain was being fried. His wife visited him a couple of times but each visit had a retrograde impact on him. He became angry and accused her of being in bed with the Devil and she was the reason he was being tortured. It was agreed it would be better if she didn't visit for the time being.

Bit by bit some normality returned to Danny and he was thought fit enough to go to the transition ward, the last stop before entering the community again. It was then thought all right for his wife to visit. He didn't talk to her but sat in his chair rocking backwards and forwards. After his wife left Danny walked out into the field beside the hospital. He started to walk around it and around it and around it. At bedtime he was still walking around the field and so was returned to the main hospital. His wife never visited again.

After further treatment Danny did eventually return to the community. He weaned himself back into life by working at a night shelter. He dealt with people that society wished it could sweep under the carpet. They were people with behavioural and alcohol problems. He thought there, but by the grace of God, he might have gone. The work gave him a sense of fulfilment without being overtaxing but there was a sense of frustration. There was nothing he could do for some, such as the ex-soldier who could not escape the deeds he'd been ordered to carry out in the Malaysian jungle. Alcohol was his escape and the best Danny could do was give him a warm bed in which to wrestle his demons.

Danny had met up over a coffee with his wife but she'd told him that the marriage was over. She told him she was still having to deal with their children's anxiety resulting from his treatment of them. On the one hand they recognised he had been ill but on the other they were too frightened to live with someone who might revert once again. They didn't feel safe and didn't want to live on that knife edge. For some reason Danny didn't feel anything, he thought he should have, but didn't. This was the woman and the children he had loved so much and would have done anything remotely possible for them. What was it that didn't bother him about his wife's decision? Was it that he'd already inwardly accepted that his marriage was over? Or was it the pills that he was taking that had anaesthetised his emotions? He didn't know.

After working at the night shelter for a while and comfortable that he wasn't going to relapse, he approached the Bishop to see if there was an opportunity to re-enter clerical life and look after a parish again. The Bishop had a soft spot for Danny but equally didn't want to put the Church at much of a risk. It was one of his adviser's that came up with the solution. There was a parish at the head of one of the dales, the church stood alone in a field in the middle of nowhere. The congregation was in decline and the current incumbent was shortly to retire. Surely Danny could do no harm there. And so he was appointed.

Danny moved into an ex-miner's cottage which was a good mile or more away from the church but was reasonably handy for the pub. He had no telephone and hot water had to be heated on the range. His parish was miles of moorland and a congregation he could have accommodated around his kitchen table. He cleaned up the church after finding beer cans strewn around and cigarettes stubbed out on the floor. After that he locked it up. He thought that one day it would become a lovely bijou country retreat for some city dweller.

His duties weren't very onerous and most nights would find him dropping into the pub to while away an hour or two with the locals. Most days would find him fishing. This was something new to him and he found it calming and relaxing. He was enjoying life.

After he'd been there awhile the game of Bishop's musical chairs took place and a new Bishop appeared in his See. The new Bishop had a sense of business and looked to use metrics to guide him in the management of his bailiwick. This was a Bishop with ambition and he was in a bit of a hurry. Danny's parish quickly fell under the Bishop's gaze. He was of the view that a surprise visit to the next Sunday service would quickly confirm his worst fears and seal the fate of the parish. Danny had a friend in the Bishop's office who rang up the pub in the upper dale to ask them to forewarn Danny of the intended visit.

The publican and the other locals set to work to support Danny. They rounded up all and sundry to attend the next church service no matter what their religious leanings might be. When Sunday came the Bishop arrived to find a very full church. After attending the service and undertaking the minimum of pleasantries he departed as quickly as he could. The Muslims in the congregation were somewhat amused by the experience and were sure that Allah would understand that they hadn't forsaken him but were undertaking a work of greater good.

Sadly, the quantum of Danny's weekly collection plate soon gave the Bishop the information he wanted and shortly after, Danny's parish was merged with a couple lower down the dale. He was advised that his services were no longer required. Danny wasn't dismayed, he'd begun to feel a fraud as he'd lost his faith long since but had been seduced by the easy and enjoyable life he'd been living. He'd gone through the motions and thought his faith might come back, but it never did.

The last Dave heard of Danny was that he had moved back down the dale and had become a furniture humper working for a removal company. He lived in a small cottage not too far from a pub and when not working was to be seen taking off with his fishing rod over his shoulder. It was rare to see him in church. He was content.

Chapter Two
What Goes Around

Dave had wandered along the High Row and took a seat where in the good old days he would have been squished by a British Road Service's lorry carrying a load of steel to one part of the country or another. British Road Services had been an unprofitable part of the British Transport Commission. In his youth Dave had worked for one of the profitable divisions of the Commission, Pickfords, in Newcastle. One day when he was in the office the Managing Director from London paid a rare visit. He was introduced to Dave who was asked what his ambitions were.

"To have your job one day," Dave replied.

"You're a cheeky bugger," was all he received by way of encouragement. The Managing Director swept into the branch manager's office and sat down. The first thing he wanted to know from the branch manager was where the Olivetti adding machine had come from. He was told that it was hired and that it had helped speed up a number of the clerical tasks in the office, as well as adding to the branch's auditability as paper slips from the machine could be attached to batches of invoices and clipped to the ledgers.

"Send it back, now," was the petulant response.

Sometime later, as part of his training, Dave had asked if he could be considered for relieving branch managers when they went on holiday. The response that time was,

"You big headed bugger."

It wasn't much after that that Dave moved on. And not much after that, his manager who was in his mid-forties, emigrated with his family to Australia. Dave thought that was a courageous move.

This flashback made Dave wonder about some of the bad managers he had come across in his life and the fact that at times company boards seemed not to see what was happening. There was one manager he recalled who would continuously restructure the company particularly if someone coming through the ranks was seen as a challenger to him. Any such threat was met with a restructured redundancy.

Thankfully, Dave was a little to one side of one of the worst managers he encountered. The Board at one of their meetings recognised that the company's performance was both profitable and consistent. The plans were more of the same but the board had seen the returns that some of the younger entrepreneurs were getting in other companies and they wanted a piece of that action. They needed someone to come in and give their company a bit of a stir up. One of the Board members said he'd heard of a young engineer who had an MBA and might be just the ticket for them. He'd apparently already sorted out a couple of companies in his career.

So it was that Bill Hazlet joined the company as a Deputy Chief Executive but with a direct line to the Board. He was to sort things out whilst the Chief Executive was charged with looking after business as usual. This was more easily said than done when systems and structures were being changed around and a Board who didn't want to know about any difficulties.

Bill quickly let it be known that it was all about him and he knew best. He knew which of the Board members he needed to cosy up to. He developed a relationship with the Chief Executive that was more by the way of informing him what he was doing rather than consulting or discussing. He appointed a couple of people who had worked for him in the past to help with the necessary restructuring. He wanted to get rid of the collegiate approach where people looked out for the interests of others. If each person concentrated on their own role that's all that was required. Each would have their own measures and that's what they would need to meet. He knew that if you could identify an eighth of a person not needed here and another eighth there then in no time at all you could get rid of a person, one person led to another and so on. He'd soon be making lots of savings, no trouble at all.

New systems were needed, first this one of the existing systems and then that one were regarded as 'dogs' and 'dogs with fleas.' He didn't know how the company managed to do business with what they had. He was also of the view that there were a number of things that just didn't need doing. There were savings everywhere in Bill's eyes.

It was at this point Bill took a particular disliking to Sid. Sid pointed out that if he chose not to do this or that then there might be adverse consequences because of the impact they could have on customers, the audit, the tax authorities or whatever. Sid was seen as a stick in the mud who objected to change. He was the sort of person the company didn't need. Bill vowed to get rid of him but not by way of making him redundant, he didn't want Sid to have the satisfaction of receiving a cent of redundancy pay.

Bill's conversations with most of the underlings he had dealings with were clipped and curt but his conversations with Sid were downright hostile. Nobody was allowed to say a good thing about Sid in his presence. They were dismissed with a snarl. Any work demanded of Sid was badly written or missed the point entirely, according to Bill. Sid had to leave his papers so Bill could do them properly. The fact that the substance was not materially changed when presented elsewhere was not lost on Sid.

It was necessary for Sid to set up meetings from time to time as part of his role. The first time it happened came as a shock and he wasn't quite sure how to handle it. He was disinvited from his own meeting and Bill took over. Bill would then not necessarily share the contents of the meeting with Sid. Indeed, that became part of Bill's way of operating, he'd withhold pertinent information only to release it when it could cause maximum embarrassment.

Sid still had a mortgage so, much as he would have liked to have told Bill to stick anything and everything sharp and pointy up his proverbial, he bit his bottom lip and persevered but the strain started to tell.

He was disappointed that some of his work colleagues, some of whom he thought he was close to, not only didn't support him but distanced themselves from him. He was even more disappointed when he could see the glee in the eye of one or two as they witnessed his discomfort. He'd done nothing to harm them so couldn't understand the vindictiveness.

On the other hand the support he received from others was a continuing motivator for him, even people who were a little remote from him held out a hand. They were surprised that the Chief Executive would allow this to happen but Sid recognised that he was in a difficult position especially with the Board listening more to Bill than him.

The strain had started to impact on Sid's marriage which just added to his problems. Sid's wife wasn't very sympathetic. She couldn't understand why he would want some time alone after a harrowing day in the office. He needed to buck himself up and take her out to the theatre, the cinema, or wherever. She'd give him alone time! She started going out regularly with her girlfriends and leaving him to his misery.

Bill couldn't resist himself. After being presented with the latest offering from Sid he dismissed it as if dealing with a used piece of toilet tissue. He went on to tell Sid he was useless, a loser who was incapable of doing anything right.

"You can't even satisfy your wife; you can't even make her happy. No wonder she's out and about." Sid was shocked and told Bill what he could do with himself.

Shortly after, Sid was offered a job by someone who knew him well. As he was leaving, the Chief Executive said he didn't want Sid to leave and hadn't realised what was going on. Sid used to have a regard for his Chief but took that with a pinch of salt. He was happy in his new job but it didn't paper over the cracks of his marriage. It was a civilised parting of the ways with each knowing they were heading down different paths in life.

After a couple of years Bill moved on to his next challenge. In his eye he had achieved so much, made savings here and efficiencies there, he'd pushed the dead wood out and the company should go on to deliver everything he had promised. If they didn't then it would obviously be because he wasn't there anymore to keep them on the straight and narrow. He'd hang up his shingle as a consultant until he landed his next job.

The people in the company sighed with relief on Bill's departure. They then set about trying to undo some of the damage. The savings had resulted in necessary things not being done. The holes had to be refilled which to some degree meant reinventing them because so much corporate knowledge had been thrown out of the door. Some of the ex-employees were happy to come back as consultants on salaries way in excess of anything they had earned when employed by the company. They lamented the old days when each had the other's back but were happy to shake their heads and take the money.

Sid had been invited to a pub quiz evening; he hadn't particularly wanted to go but his friends were insistent. It was there he met his future wife. He was at the bar ordering a round of drinks for the table when she approached the bar with an empty wine glass in her hand. He added her wine to his order and they started chatting. They immediately enjoyed each other's company and very soon one thing led to another. The complication was that she was married, not very happily but nonetheless she was married. However, the relationship flourished and she willingly divorced her husband and married Sid.

On their wedding night as they lay side by side, Sid turned to his wife with a smile on his face and gave her a kiss. She asked him if he was happy.

"Yes," he answered, "Very much so, I never thought I'd find love and happiness in my life again, but you came along and have made my life complete once more. I love you so much."

"And me you," purred the former Mrs Hazlet.

Chapter Three
The Good Luck Charm

After sitting and pondering for a while Dave decided to stretch his legs and go for a walk towards his old school. Rather than retrace the normal route he used to take, up Post House Wynd and Duke Street, he thought he'd go along the High Row to Bondgate and then up Woodlands Road.

As Dave passed the shop where Gene Fitzgerald's mother used to sell fruit he recalled working there, unloading the cases of fruit from the lorry from Hull early in the morning, stacking them high in the alleyway and then having to dash off to school, not infrequently late. Dusty, the Alsatian, spent most of his day keeping guard in a space under the counter where the till was. Dusty wasn't the type of dog you could pat, not if you wanted to keep your hand in one piece and equally, if you weren't known to him, don't put your hand anywhere near that till.

Dave occasionally was asked to take Dusty for a walk, but it was more like Dusty taking Dave for a walk. He didn't walk with a leash and went wherever he wanted to go around the streets near the shop with Dave beside him. When he was ready he'd turn his nose back towards the shop and that was the end of the walk. Dave was there merely to deter the naïve and unknowing approaching Dusty with outstretched hands muttering,

"Who's a lovely boy then?" If the contempt in Dusty's eyes wasn't sufficient giveaway then Dave had to explain that the dog didn't like being patted. The persistent would-be dog whisperer got the message that Dusty really, really, didn't like being patted when the dog went rigid and started a deep throated growl.

Dusty reminded Dave of a dog that was very similar to him in New Zealand. At the time Dave worked in an area where burglars would seize the opportunity given half a chance. The company Dave worked for had new cars in a yard so at night they had a dog patrolling it, who was on a lead on a fixed wire. The only thing that was ever stolen was the dog. The firm next door sold car parts and there the owner, who had an Alsatian just like Dusty, let his dog run free in the yard. The owner came in one morning to find an intruder cornered by the dog.

"Good morning," was all he said and continued about his business leaving the dog eyeing the intruder. The would be burglar eventually pleaded for help which is when the police were called.

Dave walked further up Woodlands Road to where Holy Trinity Church is. He had painted and sketched this church both inside and out but it was the cemetery at the rear that brought a smile to his face. It was here that Dave and some of his contemporaries used to go and hide and share a quick ciggy after they had bunked off from school. Allegedly, one of them had had sex on one of the gravestones. It didn't sound very comfortable to Dave.

It was in this part of Woodland Road that Dave felt something more than a nostalgic smile, it was a sense of warmth and a feeling of goodwill towards a wonderful group of people who had crossed his path at one point in his life. It wasn't anything to do with the church, the coterie of misfits who met in the cemetery, delightful though they were, or his school that lay just around the corner. It was the nurses, and the street leading to the nurses' home which was somewhere just across the road. Or so Dave thought. He wasn't quite so sure now with all the new buildings at the Memorial Hospital, leastwise they were new to him. He'd walked down that street so many times in the past that it seemed strange not to instantly recognise it.

Dave had got to know the nurses through his best mate's girlfriend who'd taken it upon herself to train as a nurse. Over time he'd dated more than one and had been attracted to them because of the outlook they had on life. They had encountered more suffering and death earlier in life than most. This seemed to wring any vanity from them. They liked fashionable clothes like most young women but it wasn't the be all and end all of some of their non-nursing contemporaries. They had a zest for life knowing this was their only attempt at it, and fate may intervene to make it much shorter than they might wish. They had a confidence, vitality and equally compassion with empathy. Yet, there were the times that their confidence faltered and an unexpected or unfair death or prolonged suffering of a patient dented the resilience that no party was going to repair either on that night or for a while to come. But they had a job to do and they rebounded, they had to. Dave reflected on what a glorious bunch of self-assured young women they were. Yet, sadly, this didn't carry all of them through life.

The last time Dave had seen Janice she was just beginning to build her confidence back. She'd started a job as a clerk at a car dealership but still didn't want too much responsibility. She didn't feel that she could hop on a train by herself and visit London, all those people, those overpowering skyscrapers, it would be too much for her, she just knew she couldn't cope. She was happy with her set routines and a limited world.

Shortly after Janice had qualified as a nurse she had met Les. He was a motor mechanic. She thought him smart and handsome and had ambition since he wanted to start his own garage. He was tall, protective and funny. Very quickly she fell in love and seemingly he with her. They made love whenever the opportunity would allow.

They got married a couple of years after they had started going out. It was a white wedding without being too lavish. Some of the friends that Janice would have liked to have had there didn't receive an invitation at Les' insistence. Les had been protective of Janice and had taken an interest in her friends and suggested from time to time that she should stop seeing this one or that one for some reason or another. Janice realised that Les was looking after her and she was grateful for the stories he had to tell her that made sure she was being kept out of harm's way.

The wedding night came as a surprise to her, as they were heading towards the bed with love in their eyes Les suddenly punched Janice in the stomach. She crumpled up breathlessly in pain. Les put a hand around her neck and drew his head quite close to hers,

"Don't you ever be unfaithful," he hissed through the ugliest of faces Janice had ever seen on Les. He pushed her in the direction of the bed. Janice crawled onto the bed in shock and tried to get her breath back through her sobs. As she crawled up into a ball to give herself some relief Les was upon her again.

"I'm sorry, I'm so sorry, I didn't mean to do that. I'm so sorry, I love you so much, I didn't mean to do that." Les kept repeating his apology as he tried to shower kisses on her wherever he could. His persistence ended up with them having sex whilst Janice tried to suppress her discomfort.

The next day as they went for a walk down by the river near their honeymoon hotel Les continued to apologise to Janice and promised, cross his heart, that nothing like that would ever happen again.

The rest of the honeymoon saw Les being so attentive, loving and caring to Janice that at the end of it she almost doubted what had happened on the wedding night; had she been dreaming? But she knew she hadn't. When talking to older patients who had tripped and fractured a bone, they had spoken of losing self confidence in doing things as simple as walking. For the first time she had some understanding of what they meant.

After the honeymoon they had returned to the bungalow they had bought on the edge of town. At the same time, Les had started his own business, in a garage he had rented. As he was busy setting up his new business while doing some renovations on the bungalow in the evenings, he said he didn't want anybody calling to see them.

Les could be moody at times and he didn't like Janice catching up with her colleagues after work. He liked his dinner on the table when he came in from the garage, which could be at varying times. If the food was shrivelled up from being kept warm for a long time then he'd criticise her cooking. He suggested that Janice get shifts at the hospital so that she was there when he wanted her. After all he was there to look after her so she should look after him.

Janice took her wedding vows seriously, for better or worse she had pledged. She thought that it must be her fault that Les was a bit grumpy at times. She knew this must be the case because at other times Les could be his smiling, happy, caring self. It was lovely when he was like that, they would make love like there was no tomorrow. Yet, at other times, she wondered what she had done wrong.

When the garage failed it meant they could no longer afford to live in the bungalow they had bought. It had to be sold to pay their debts. They moved to a two up and two down terraced house in the north of the town. Les said they had to go somewhere where nobody knew them. Janice was determined to stand by her man.

Les told Janice not to talk about what had happened to anyone, it was no one's business but theirs. Everyone could keep their sticky beaks out of their affairs. Janice assured him she wouldn't think of discussing it with anyone, not even her mother.

"Particularly not her," spat Les.

Life in the new home left Janice more isolated than ever. Les had easily found a job with one of the larger garages and occasionally went for a quick drink with his new workmates when they'd finished their shift. Janice never knew whether he'd be going for a drink that particular day or not. Food was expected on the table when he came through the door. Les had no tolerance if Janice had to work past her shift a little bit because of an emergency or her replacement had called in sick. Her first priority was him. Any divergence could easily result in a savage verbal lashing.

But not always. There were times when Les was understanding, loving and caring. She didn't have to worry if she was a little late, after all these things happen and it was good she was so conscientious. Which may explain why Janice thought it was her fault when things didn't go quite right.

Les said that people were laughing behind his back because he obviously couldn't afford to keep his wife. That's why she was forced to go out to work. He didn't want to listen to Janice's plea that she enjoyed going out to work and not only that it was doing a worthwhile job. That's not what people were saying behind his back. It had to stop. She had to stop.

She definitely had to stop after she told Les in one of his more benevolent moods that one of the patients had made a pass at her. This instantly turned the switch from benevolence to malevolence. She must have courted the attention; she was a slut. Les didn't want his wife putting herself about like that. She should be ashamed.

Shortly after she stopped working, Les closed their joint bank account and transferred all the money into a sole account he'd opened in his name, after all he was earning all the money now, it was his. He gave her an allowance each week to buy groceries but it was barely adequate. There was nothing left over for her to spend on herself.

She was there for his pleasure and sometimes his pleasure was on the dining table straight after a meal. She was thankful she had never become pregnant and hoped her precautions would never fail her.

The bouts of verbal abuse continued and seemed to become more frequent. He'd explain in a sort of apologetic way afterwards that if she behaved herself and looked after him properly all the time then none of this would happen. She had to understand it was her fault. She knew that.

The verbal abuse was now sometimes accompanied by physical abuse, nothing to be seen, but punches and savage nips to the body, above the knee and below the neck. Janice wondered what she could do to make the good times last. She tried her hardest.

She seldom went out other than to do the shopping. There was nothing to go out for. She avoided the neighbours as she felt guilty, she wasn't quite sure what for, but she felt guilty. She didn't want to catch their eyes and they had got used to looking at her from a distance shaking their heads in sympathy.

Les started going out more and more for a drink. When he did it was hard to know what his mood would be on his return. From time to time she was sure she could smell the scent of another woman on him. She'd once raised the topic with him. Only to be asked if she could blame him? Had she looked in the mirror lately? She was a sloven, she should be pleased he gave her house room. If she didn't behave she'd soon know 'what was what' and find herself out on the street. So, Janice lived for the good times reminding herself of her marriage vows.

It was close to Christmas and Janice took it upon herself to make a Christmas pudding. It was a fiddly thing to make and she knew it would take quite a bit of steaming before it was ready for being cooked again on Christmas Day. In the final mix Janice added a silver threepenny bit that her grandmother had given her many years ago, a lucky silver threepenny bit. Then she tied a cloth over the top of the basin and put it in a steamer and left it to burble and happily hiss away. All this was going on while Les was out doing whatever he did. When he returned he'd obviously had a drink or two.

"What's that you've been cooking?" he asked.

"It's a pudding for Christmas." Janice replied

"That smells good," said Les sniffing the air, "I'll have a bit of that now."

"But it's for Christmas," protested Janice, "I've spent ages making it."

"Have you made any custard?" said Les, ignoring Janice's protest.

"But it's for Christmas," said Janice almost in tears.

"Some custard, now," commanded Les, "or you and me will be having words."

Janice knew better. She made some custard and put it into a jug. She put this, the pudding, a bowl and spoon in front of Les. With tears silently flowing down her face she closed the door just as he was ripping the cloth off the top of the pudding basin. She went up the stairs to bed feeling tentative about what the rest of the night might hold.

Curled up in the foetal position she waited for the onslaught but sleep overcame her. When she woke up it was morning. It felt strange, Les was not in bed with her. Had he come and gone without her knowing?

It was a chilly morning so she quickly refreshed herself in the bathroom and dressed. She went downstairs with the thought of a warm cup of tea to start her day. As she opened the door that she'd firmly closed last night, she was startled to see the table overturned with custard and pudding strewn about and there was Les stretched out holding his throat. She didn't need her nursing experience to see Les was as dead as a dodo. She was shocked and not quite sure what she should do. If Les had allowed a telephone in the house maybe she would have rung someone for help but there wasn't one. She decided she'd better take herself off to the nearest phone box. She was nervous about doing this. As she walked there she couldn't work out her emotions. There was sadness and guilt, after all she had heard a bit of a kerfuffle from the room below after she had tucked herself up in bed. Knowing Les was in a bit of a belligerent mood she was in no hurry to go and investigate. She hated to admit it but noticed there was a bit of a lightness in her step as she headed to the phone box. It wasn't joy but Janice wondered if there was a guilty sense of relief creeping up on her.

The post mortem revealed that Les had chocked on a silver threepenny bit lodged in his throat. Janice's lucky silver threepenny piece. She had wondered about asking for it back but hoped she would never have need of it again, so thought better of it.

Dave had been pleased to hear that Janice had picked up her self-esteem and confidence once more but it had taken years rather than weeks for that to happen.

Chapter Four
Be Careful What You Chew On

Being near the Nurses Home, Dave was dwelling on his attempts to impress the opposite sex when he was younger. He'd fallen very much in love and was wanting to impress his girlfriend. He would have liked to have wined and dined her in a nice restaurant however, he didn't have much money. He was between occupations at the time having found out there wasn't much meaning in life trying to be a door to door salesman selling plastic bags.

After much thought Dave decided to invest the little discretionary cash that he had that week in a couple of eggs, an onion, some rice and a small tin of shrimps. He would entertain his girlfriend at his digs and treat her to a plate of shrimp fried rice. All savoured with the finest glass of water that the tap could provide.

The day of the grand occasion dawned and Chef Dave's confidence was as big as his smile. His girlfriend could sit and watch as he displayed his culinary expertise. In one pan he boiled the water and put in the rice whilst in another he fried the eggs as an omelette so they could be cut up and added to the rice in due course along with the cooked onion. When the rice was cooked he drained it, added a generous helping of cooking oil to the pan before putting the rice back in along with the other ingredients. The valuable lesson Dave learned that day was never to fry freshly cooked rice. If you do never try to present it as fried rice. Rice a là stodgy glug would be the nearest descriptor. His girlfriend politely picked out the odd shrimp here and there to chew on at great length before declaring herself fully satiated and profusely thanked him for trying before hurrying home via the fish and chip shop.

Dave consoled himself with knowing he wasn't alone when it came to culinary disasters. Indeed his girlfriend had tried to impress him with her zabaglione making skills. This wonderful Italian creation of egg yolks, sugar and Marsala wine is nectar on the tastebuds, unless of course you substitute salt for the sugar. Dave felt he had no choice but to agree with her that it was a simple mistake that anyone could make when the salt and sugar were stored in identical storage jars on the same shelf.

When it came to haute cuisine Dave knew full well his mother could have her moments. She worked in a large works canteen which offered a selection of dishes to the workers and so he assumed she had a reasonable wide knowledge of diverse types of food. One day Dave had one of his avant-garde moments. He fancied a change from the usual fare of meat and two well boiled vegetables and he'd requested his mother, for the first time, to make him a chicken curry with rice. The chicken curry was fine unfortunately, the rice came in the form of a rice pudding. He never picked up the courage to ask her for a sweet and sour dish, he just couldn't face the thought of a jelly bean stuck in the middle of a lemon.

The chicken curry was almost matched by one that Dave had ordered in a hotel in Hamilton, New Zealand. The curry was served with mashed potatoes, carrots and boiled cabbage. Shakespeare wrote,'If music be the food of love then play on,' but Dave wasn't sure what he'd have written if he'd been confronted with the chicken curry and the shrimp fried rice.

Was it the thought of love that reminded Dave of Frankie or was he still thinking of Janice and her lucky silver threepence. Both women had experienced violence in their lives. It was a little later in his career when Dave met Frankie, she was a woman who had worked in his team. It was getting towards the end of the financial year so a variety of tasks needed to be undertaken and all within a tight timeframe. This required Frankie to work overtime to meet her deadline. The nature of the work meant only she could undertake this particular task as there was no other relief immediately to hand. She was very good at what she did. There were other people working in the building so Dave felt comfortable leaving her to her work. As he was departing the office Dave said, rather flippantly,

"I must love you and leave you."

"Nobody's ever told me they love me before," Frankie replied. Dave felt rather sad for her knowing full well that she'd had a troubled background.

Frankie was very distinctive, her choice of clothing was flamboyant, some even found it challenging. Probably the best, almost contradictory, description would be that she dressed in brightly coloured punk gothic. Her medium to long hair reflected the clothes she wore having stripes of vibrant colours that changed on a regular basis. From time to time parts of her cranium were shaved. She sported some tattoos but the interesting one was one Dave had only ever heard about. It was a serpent wrapped around her upper thigh with its tail disappearing between her legs. Frankie had incredibly smelly feet and Dave preferred sitting up wind of her at a meeting.

Frankie was married to a biker, Zed. Dave surmised from what had been said that in terms of love, Frankie came a long way behind Zed's first love, his Harley Davidson. Zed was not very hirsute; he admired the long flowing beards of ZZ Top but knew he could never aspire to such facial magnificence. It is said that it was this deficiency that led him to want to prove himself against all others. He was known for his violence, some thought he was a psychopath.

During the time Frankie worked for Dave she would regale his team, usually at the Monday morning tea break, with stories of daring-do that she and Zed had got up to at the weekend. From the innuendo of making love on a motor bike speeding down a highway to stories of wild parties and outrunning speed cops. At the weekends, her life appeared to be very lascivious. Dave was never quite sure how much to believe.

From time to time, after her weekend jaunts, Frankie would sport a variety of grazes, cuts and bruises. Each abrasion would be accompanied by stories of crashes, near crashes and Zed laying down his bike, in other words dropping the motorbike on its side to slide along and avoid an inevitable crash. There were graphic details of Frankie somersaulting over the bonnets of cars to miraculously land in such a way that she suffered no serious harm, or of sliding along the road and hitting her head on the kerb and being knocked out. When she came too she had realised how she'd been saved by her helmet and she was able to walk away with a smile on her face.

Dave wasn't always convinced that some of the injuries she displayed were in congruence with the stories she related, but who was he to argue. After all, Frankie told the stories with great gusto and with a smile on her face. Dave couldn't fully relate to Frankie's hedonistic lifestyle.

Frankie didn't turn up for work for a couple of days. Unusually, for her there was no communication, no proffered excuses. Dave enquired from her colleagues but they'd heard nothing either. When she turned up for work she sported a couple of black eyes and other signs that she had been badly beaten. She was very subdued and went to her desk, put her head down and got on with her work. She avoided any interaction with her colleagues and questions of concern were met with,

"I don't want to talk about it." It had the impact of subduing the rest of the office. Her colleagues wanted to help but didn't know what to do.

Dave was very concerned for her and asked to see her in his office. She avoided or ignored the first couple of requests but eventually had no option when Dave stood by her desk and insisted. She followed him to his office with her head bowed down. For obvious reasons her exuberance had deserted her.

Dave wasted no time; it was obvious to him as to what had happened to Frankie and he wasn't going to beat about the bush. If he wasn't right about his assumptions than he had no doubt that Frankie would put him straight.

"You don't have to put up with behaviour like that. It isn't right for you to be beaten up. There are things we can do to help you. There are people we can refer you to. We can look at getting restraining orders to help you." After a long pause Frankie said she was alright and she could manage OK, thank you.

"If you'd rather not speak to me," Dave persisted, "can I get somebody you'd be more comfortable talking to, another woman perhaps."

"No, I'm alright," said Frankie talking to her feet.

"Given your obvious injuries, can I get you any medical help?" continued Dave trying to find some little niche that could lead to her receiving the help she obviously needed. Everything that Dave tried was stonewalled. Eventually, he had to leave the conversation with,

"If there is anything I can do, please let me know."

Dave contacted the Police but was told they really couldn't help unless she complained to them. In talking to her closest colleagues he was told that she had clammed up with them as well. Women's Refuge said all you could do at this stage was keep an eye on her and offer support when and where necessary. They were happy to have a counsellor talk to her if she was willing.

Over the next couple of weeks Dave tried more than once to talk to Frankie to reinforce that she should not accept or tolerate anybody beating her up. He told her that if it had happened once it would likely happen again and she was best to seek advice and consider her options. On one last attempt Frankie opened up a little.

"Everything's alright now," she said, "Zed and I have settled down again. He got angry because we'd gone to a party and I decided to leave early so I grabbed a cab and went home without him. And please, I don't want to talk about it again." Dave reiterated his message that family violence wasn't acceptable and if it should happen again please let him know as he knew people he could put her in contact with to help.

There the matter rested. Over the course of time Dave's career took him in one direction and Frankie's in another.

Occasionally, Dave saw Frankie in the street but, for whatever reason, she chose to ignore him and pass by with her head down.

A couple of years later Dave bumped into an old friend. They hadn't seen each other for a while so there was a lot of catching up to do which was done over a coffee at the nearest bistro. As his friend was a Harley owner Dave suspected he may have come across Frankie.

"Yes I know her,"

"How's her marriage?" Dave enquired.

"She's divorced now," replied the friend.

"I'm pleased for her sake," said Dave. He then went on to tell his friend about the time she was beaten up for the audacity of taking a cab home from a party by herself.

"I think that must have been the party over at Eastbourne which I also attended." The friend went on to elucidate. "We had to separate Zed and Frankie who were having an argument. Whilst some engaged with Zed, the rest of us pushed Frankie into a cab that we'd flagged down."

"So, there was a bit more of a background than I was led to believe," said Dave.

"Indeed, the party had been going quite well until Zed decided he needed a bit of fresh air. He stepped out the back and discovered Frankie with another man. In many circumstances there might have been any number of credible reasons why this could be something totally innocuous. Unfortunately, for Frankie, this wasn't one of those occasions, as she was caught in fellatio."

Chapter Five

Patience Is Rewarded

Being somewhere near where the nurses' home had been, Dave ruminated that on the whole the nurses had been a delightful, no nonsense practical bunch.

Being a nurses' home, the location did, from time to time, attract the occasional pervert and weirdo. On one occasion one of these cranks took to knocking on the windows of the ground floor bedrooms. The response from one of the occupants was,

"If you're handsome come in, if not get lost." On another occasion a peeping tom was confronted by some of the nurses. The man faced them and opened up his raincoat to expose himself. The nurses were unimpressed.

"Put it away, we've seen better," said one of them. The flasher scurried away.

Dave did recall that at one point the nurses' home did get the reputation of being a knocking shop, but not in the sense of a bordello. Once again the home had been annoyed by yet another peeping tom. On this occasion the nurses had come up with a system of knocking on their radiator pipes to warn each other that he was about. One night the sister-in-charge had heard this and had phoned the police who responded promptly and had the offender in handcuffs in short order.

Dave knew that the nurses could have that 'don't mess with me' outlook. Patience was one such nurse. Like a lot of the nurses she had in time found her beau, fallen in love, got married and settled down. They bought and had moved into one of the newer houses in the Mowden Estate. Her bliss and contentment continued for a few years and then she began to wonder. The late nights her husband, Phil, had to work started to have a regular pattern about them rather than being occasional and haphazard as they used to be.

"It comes with the added responsibility that I have," Phil had told her. Patience wondered if she was becoming a bit neurotic or maybe just becoming a bit silly.

He used to take her with him when, from time to time, he had to travel for his work. They used to make a long weekend of it where possible. Maybe there was just a bit of staleness coming into the marriage. Patience thought perhaps she should add a bit of a spark. She went out and bought some sexier nightwear, not that there was anything wrong with their love making. Indeed on that front there had been a bit more vigour and enthusiasm about it lately, but somehow those tiny little touches of tenderness seemed to be missing.

Patience decided she was just being stupid. There it may have ended except one day she was having a coffee with a friend of hers. For some reason they came around to the subject of marriages and relationships. Her friend observed that she thought a discreet affair helped add a little spice to a marriage and kept it fresh and interesting. She also thought it helped in bed. Patience could not agree, a marriage was about trust and faithfulness between two people, break that trust and for her the relationship was broken.

Patience's doubts came back to her on her birthday. She had seen a charge going through their credit card statement for a local jewellers. She thought she was going to receive a nice surprise for her birthday. Indeed there was a surprise, Phil gave her a box of chocolates and some flowers.

A couple of days later she casually enquired about the charge on their credit card. Phil assured her it had been wrongly charged to them and he was chasing it up to have the transaction reversed. He told her not to bother about looking after the credit card charges as he had it all in hand.

On the one hand everything seemed in order, but on the other Patience just had this feeling that things weren't quite right. Phil seemed to have a subtle evasiveness about him but nothing she could put her finger on. He didn't smell of another woman's perfume, there were no clandestine phone calls made in the garden, or at least of which she was aware. As she told herself yet again, she was being stupid. That was until she found a strand of long auburn hair on his scarf. It wasn't hers that was for sure. It was no use asking Phil, he'd only dismiss it with some excuse. Patience thought there could be some substance to her suspicions. She hoped not, she loved Phil and she loved her life. If only this element of doubt would go away but it was pestering her like an earworm, that same old tune going over and over again in her mind. Why wouldn't it stop?

The next time Phil said he was working late she decided she'd support him and go to his office; she took him a bottle of beer and some cheese and crackers. Leastwise that was her excuse. When she got there, the office was locked up with no lights on.

She drove home and waited for Phil. When he arrived at the house she gave him the beer and some cheese and crackers ahead of his dinner. In response to Patience's concerns about him having to work so hard and so late, Phil told her about the burden of working in the office late at night. He had been all by himself while the rest of the staff were either at home with their families or out on the town but he had responsibilities and couldn't ignore them. He was ready for bed as soon as he'd eaten, he said working under the neon lights gave him a headache. Patience sympathised and gave him a couple of paracetamol.

Patience's stomach churned; she now knew that there seemed to be some substance to her suspicions. She hoped beyond hope that she was wrong and that there was a logical explanation. She couldn't imagine what it could be, but prayed there was one.

Patience needed to know but wasn't sure how to set about obtaining proof one way or the other. She could just front up to Phil but, if he was already living a lie, then she may not learn the truth. If there really was nothing to it then she endangered their relationship by the very act of asking. There was no one she knew well enough at Phil's office whom she could ask without it getting back to Phil and she certainly wasn't going to ask his family or close friends. She was lost at the moment as to what to do next.

Patience continued life as normal but at the back of her mind she wasn't sure it was normal. As part of life with Phil she had become used to cooking for him, doing his laundry and generally looking after him. As part of this she noticed one of his suits had had something spilled on it and took it upon herself to take it to the dry cleaners. Out of habit she went through the pockets to make sure nothing was left in them. On the inside pocket she found a receipt from a hotel, it was for a king-size room. That in itself didn't concern her but what did make her raise her eyebrows was the breakfast for two. She needed to know if he was being unfaithful, but how?

She took the opportunity a few weeks later. One of Phil's weekend conferences was coming up, he would have loved to have taken Patience but it was going to be work, work and work. It wouldn't be fun plus he had to look after some clients. Discretely and under an assumed name, Patience booked herself into the same hotel and asked to have a room away from those booked for any conferences they were holding. She explained that she didn't want to be disturbed by the antics that delegates sometimes got up to.

When the day of the conference came around Patience did her best to try and disguise herself with a scarf, pulled back hair and sun glasses. She dressed in some clothes she'd carefully selected from the Salvation Army thrift shop although, she suspected she could have worn a number of items out of her wardrobe and Phil would have been none the wiser. She jumped into a hire car and headed for the hotel.

She'd found out when the introductory cocktail party was scheduled on Phil's programme and chose that time to book in. As she did she enquired about her friend Phil's room number, using his surname, so she could contact him once she'd settled in.

The next morning Patience used room service for her breakfast and waited until the conference had started for the day before taking herself off shopping. She returned to the hotel in mid-afternoon and reconnoitred where Phil's room was before returning to her own room to refresh herself. The hotel lounge was large enough to be secreted in but not too large that she couldn't see what was going on. Just before the conference ended for the day Patience established herself in a quiet corner of the lounge with a drink and hid behind sunglasses and a newspaper.

The conference attendees emerged in due course with quite a large number of them heading to the bar in the lounge. Many stood around the bar talking to each other while groups started to seat themselves at tables. Patience was surreptitiously keeping an eye out for Phil but hadn't spotted him. She began to wonder if she'd called it wrong, she also wondered how much longer she could nurse her drink. She didn't want to go to the bar again and risk running into Phil. Then she saw him at the far side of a group talking animatedly standing by the bar. Beside him was Eva. She'd met Eva and her husband, Simon, at the firm's Christmas do.

Patience would have liked to have stared but disciplined herself to occasional peeks and sideways glances. The little of the behaviour she could detect seemed to suggest they seemed to be more than work colleagues. It was the way they looked at each other and the way they touched. Patience was sure. She'd wondered in the past of what she would feel like if her suspicions proved to be true. She surprised herself, she thought she might break down into hysteria, despair, regret and betrayal, but that wasn't the case. She felt an icily cold calm with an underlying searing anger. She quietly exited the lounge using a side door.

There was just one more thing to do to make sure she was totally certain, but that could wait for a little while. She had dinner in her room, set her alarm and took a little nap. At 3 o'clock in the morning she took up a position tucked away near the cleaner's cupboard by the floor's ice machine and satisfied herself that she had a good view of Phil's room. She also, reconfirmed that the fire exit was in the opposite direction to where she was hiding. She then broke the fire alarm glass and waited as the alarm bells sounded. Bleary eyed occupants of the hotel rooms started to emerge begrudgingly in a variety of déshabillé and complained to each other as they headed towards the fire exit. Then, what Patience had been waiting for happened. Phil held the door as Eva exited his room. Now Patience was certain. Knowing there was no true alarm, she headed off in a different direction and back to her own room to snuggle down in a warm bed. She reckoned that not everyone needed to have their extremities frozen off in the early hours of the morning particularly as she needed to be firing on all cylinders when she woke up. She had plans to make.

Patience waited until the conference was well underway that morning before booking herself out. She paid by cash to help protect her anonymity and returned home.

When Phil turned up that evening, following the end of the conference, Patience listened to his tales about the trials and tribulations he'd suffered that weekend. She secretly admired his story telling but did give him full marks for the accurate reporting of the false fire alarm even if he did leave out a particular detail.

It was a couple of days later that Patience had everything in place. She took the day off work to be there when the locks on their house were changed. She transferred most of their money from their joint bank account to one she had set up solely in her name. She packed a suitcase for Phil as if he was going off to one of his conferences. She took it down to his office and marched in uninvited. Phil looked quizzical when she set the suitcase down. She wished him and Eva well, walked out and went home.

Patience knew she'd have to surrender Phil's share in the

house and in the bank accounts in due course but not in the meantime. She hoped it would cause him some pain and a great deal of inconvenience. A small recompense she thought.

Patience hadn't been home too long when Phil turned up. He soon learned that his keys no longer worked. He hammered on the door and did quite a bit of yelling and cursing. Patience merely closed the curtains at the window. It was symbolic of shutting him out of her life. She hoped he got the message. After what seemed hours, peace returned to the neighbourhood. Phil had gone, the neighbours who had come out to see what all the fuss was about had gone back in. Once it was quiet, Jane, one the neighbours she was friends with, came over to check Patience was alright. Over a glass of wine Patience told her about Phil and his affair with Eva. Jane was flabbergasted, and particularly so with Eva whom she had known since school days. Whilst they were chatting away the phone kept ringing but Patience chose to ignore it.

When Patience was alone, again the phone rang for the umpteenth time. She decided to answer it and tell Phil to stop bothering her. To her surprise it was a woman's voice, it was a tearful, remorseful Eva. She apologised for what she'd done, she hadn't meant it to happen, she was so sorry. She pleaded with Patience not to tell her husband for the sake of their children.

"Please, please, don't tell my husband," she repeated. Patience hung up on her.

At first Patience felt some benevolence towards Eva but more and more wondered why she, herself, should be the only one who was to suffer from this affair. The barbs with Phil via the solicitors had started. Eva was continuing with life as if nothing had happened. She still worked at the same firm as Phil but Patience didn't know if the affair was continuing. There just seemed no consequences for her and that didn't seem right.

Her indignity increased over a glass or two of wine with Jane as she talked about 'that woman'. Patience's sense of injustice increased when Jane had said that she'd heard that Eva and her husband had gone on holiday down to Torquay. How could Eva carry on as if nothing had happened wondered Patience. It wasn't fair. After Jane had returned home, Patience stewed a bit more. Then she started ringing hotels in Torquay. After a dozen or more tries she found the hotel where Eva and her husband were staying. She asked to be put through to the husband, using his last name. He answered fairly promptly.

"Hello Simon, I'm Patience, do you know your wife has been having an affair with my husband?" She was taken aback by his response,

"How dare you ring our hotel and spoil our holiday?" Simon promptly hung up. Patience was completely knocked back.

Patience did subsequently hear that once Simon and Eva returned from holiday, Simon had marched into Phil's office and given him a black eye. Eva left the firm at the same time. Patience resigned herself to the fact that Eva was one of those Teflon women walking through life creating chaos and confusion without any bit of it coming home to roost.

As Patience had expected she had to sell the house as part of the divorce settlement. She realised sufficient funds, together with a manageable mortgage, to be able buy herself a terraced house just off Corporation Road. From there she set about building a new life, with her past behind her.

And so it may have remained if it wasn't for a chance encounter. She had gone to meet Marjorie, an old friend of hers, for a bar lunch. Marjorie was a woman who liked men, but on her terms. She'd once thought about marrying but had traded in the idea for a motor bike. Men came and men went. She had a certain charisma and knew if she entered a room full of men she could come out of it with at least one date, if she was of a mind. Men had their uses but she hadn't met one yet for whom she'd compromise her freedom.

Patience had seen Simon was at a table of men further over in the bar. She gave a derisive snort and mentioned it to Marjorie. Marjorie took a sneak peep and observed she had seen worse specimens. As the meal progressed Marjorie excused herself to go to the bathroom. Patience smiled to herself as she knew what a sensation Marjorie could create even by undertaking such a simple necessity. For most people it was a non-event coming and going to the toilet with the likelihood that the absence of some wouldn't even be noticed, but not for Marjorie.

Marjorie didn't walk, she had a subtle sashay of such sexual innuendo that even women couldn't ignore it. Men forgot what they were talking about, they nudged each other, they looked, some gawped and some were decidedly slack mouthed. The heads turned in unison fixed on her derriere. Her passing by seemed to have the same effect of the swinging watch of the hypnotist. Marjorie was well aware of the sensation she created but pretended to be totally unaware bordering on the aloof. If Marjorie had been carrying the train at William and Kate's wedding, people, well men at least, would have completely forgotten who was married that day and as for Kate's sister, she was an amateur. Patience smiled at Marjorie's performance.

She noticed Simon was following Marjorie's every move like all the other men at his table and then ..... and then, she noticed it. It wasn't quite like all the other men. It was no more than a tick at the side of the eye, a quiver at the corner of the mouth, the stare was more like a leer. That nuance was unmistakable, it was out and out lust that she could detect. At last she knew she would have her revenge.

Chapter Six
I Cannot Tell a Lie

The last Dave had heard of Patience, she had, after a very long relationship, remarried. He'd only ever encountered Marjorie at a distance, but was aware she had become known as the Black Widow because of her reputation to eat and spit out her partners. Her reputation didn't stop men from wanting to date her.

As Dave looked up Woodlands Road towards Cockerton, thinking of libidinous singletons, he was reminded of a relative of his who lived further up that way. Henry was regarded as handsome and he was a natty dresser. He liked his Saturday nights out on the town. He was an unashamed womaniser. He'd married more than once. Dave suspected that it was his first wife who had made an ill choice but after that all the ill choices seemed to be Henrys. Henry's first wife may well have agreed with this view, she regarded all her successors as tarts. After each relationship Henry seemed to be like a cork in water always bouncing back to the surface. Very little seemed to phase his jauntiness.

As the years rolled on nothing seemed to change about Henry, he still fancied himself and still fancied women. He did admit that once his birthdays saw him on the wrong side of seventy, women in their thirties no longer appeared to be attracted to him. In reality Henry had to admit this had been coming on for a few years before then. Notwithstanding, he was still attracted to women of that age range, more so if they were brunettes. Despite his bonhomie Henry did find himself feeling lonely.

Henry didn't want to recognise it but he had become a bit of a joke in a couple of his local bars. Women had become used to ignoring his winks and making sure there was sufficient distance between their backsides and his hands. He was the master of double-entendres that were cast out regularly like a fly fisherman with his rod. There was always the hope that he might catch something. To those who were used to him, Handy Henry could be a laugh. But to those who hadn't encountered him before, he could easily be seen as a pervert, particularly when he put his hand in his trouser pocket and enthusiastically juggled things around a bit.

One day he was in his local for a quiet pint when a couple of a young girls in their late teens started to wink at him and blow him exaggerated kisses. They were in fits of laughter as they made fun at his expense. Henry wasn't sure what he'd done to deserve this treatment and felt a mixture of anger and discomfort. He didn't stay for a second pint.

Henry didn't want a repeat of having the mickey taken out of him so tended to visit one of the villages just outside of Darlo when he wanted a drink. It was there he met Sharlene. He'd noticed her immediately as he ordered his drink from her.

"-- And one for yourself," he'd quickly added to his order.

It wasn't too busy that particular night and he'd propped himself up at the bar. Sharlene had taken Henry up on his offer and poured herself a glass of wine. She put it on the bar near where Henry was standing and when she wasn't serving she'd stop for a sip from her glass and started chatting to Henry.

Sharlene was close to Henry's ideal, she was in her late thirties, a brunette and with a shapely figure, maybe just a little bit meatier than Henry's perfect woman but not too bad for all of that. She wore a skirt and blouse to perfection but even more, Henry had noticed her legs. She was wearing nylon stockings with a seam running straight up the backs of each one of them. When she crouched down for the crisps on the bottom shelf he could detect just a hint of stocking top. Henry felt himself more than ever attracted.

Yet for all her very physical attributes, and they were certainly having a favourable impact on him, it was her voice that won him over and had him instantly in love. Her voice was honey to him, Sharlene could have read him a telephone directory and it would have been music to his ears and he would have wholeheartedly agreed with everything that she said.

Having said that the early conversation between them was the usual quite banal conversation that strangers have when encountering each other briefly, during their passage through life. They touched on the weather, the scandals and idiocies of local and national politics and the stupidities of the latest bureaucratic muddle that was creating chaos and confusion somewhere or other. He wasn't listening too much to what she had to say but just to the timbre of her voice.

The conversation started to become more personal with the exchange of names. They started to find they had things in common, areas in the locale, films, types of food, and even an interest in porcelain. They found much they were in excited agreement about. Before Henry left that night to catch his pre-arranged taxi ride home, he suggested he'd call back in a couple of days when she was on midday duty. She welcomed that, she thought it would be nice.

So it was that a couple of days later, shortly after 1.00pm, Henry arrived at the pub where Sharlene worked and if he was not exactly dancing like Nureyev, there was certainly a new found spring in his step. He settled himself at the bar and bought Sharlene a drink which she placed near him as before. Once again they talked in between her serving duties. She told him she was knocking off at 2 o'clock and they agreed to go for a walk afterwards.

They crossed over the road walked down beside the church and were soon walking beside the river. As they walked Henry took Sharlene's hand and she didn't object. They walked and talked and enjoyed each other's company and smiled a lot at each other.

The first walk ended with a peck on the cheek. The next ended with a kiss more initiated by Sharlene then Henry. The walk after that was punctuated with kisses. A couple of walks later saw Sharlene inviting Henry back for a coffee to the cottage she was renting in the village. Henry was definitely in love.

A few more visits later to the cottage and Henry found himself in bed with Sharlene. He was in seventh heaven. He would like to have seen more of her but as she led a busy life they only managed to catch up a couple of times a week. Henry had invited Sharlene back to his place, so sometimes she came there and sometimes he found himself in her cottage.

The romance progressed for a few months and whilst they had much in common it equally started to become apparent that they also had a lot not in common. The pop music of Sharlene's teenage years not only had no appeal to Henry but could lead to him becoming irritated by it. If they went for a more robust walk over the moors Sharlene found herself having to wait whilst an out of breath Henry caught up with her. Sadly, Henry could see that the romance was beginning to run its course. A shame because when things were going right Henry couldn't have been happier. Unfortunately, the not going so right days were becoming more frequent but he still wanted to hang on to the relationship.

There was an inevitability about the day when it came. They had gone for a walk by the river once more. This time Sharlene looked serious and wasn't smiling. She told Henry she liked him and they'd had great fun but the age gap was just too great and it wasn't going to work out between them. She hoped they could remain friends. Henry accepted what she had to say. On the one hand he knew what she had to say was true, on the other hand he had been thinking of proposing marriage to her with the hope that it would bring back some of the old magic. He said that all he would want for her was to be happy. They parted with a peck on the cheek and a strained smile. He was sorry it had come to an end.

Three weeks later Sharlene turned up on his doorstep. Henry was full of hope and anticipation and hadn't expected what Sharlene had to say. She told him she was pregnant. Being an old fashioned sort of bloke Henry immediately wanted to do the right thing and suggested they should get married. Sharlene thanked him but, with some hesitation, declined his offer. She said she'd come as she thought he should know about the baby. She was going away to have it as she didn't want the tittle tattle that would surround her if she stayed in the village. Henry understood and asked what he could do to help her, it was his baby as well, surely there was something he could do to support her.

Sharlene was pleased that Henry recognised his responsibilities. She said that he would well know that she'd have to fork out for nappies, clothes, a cot and what have you. She'd be grateful for a little help to defray those costs, and being he was the father paying a little child support wouldn't come amiss. Henry was sweet talked by Sharlene into promising to pay an agreed amount each week into her bank account. She went away happy and gave Henry a kiss to remember her by as she left.

Henry wore his child support like a medal of honour. Back in his local after a couple of pints he'd declare,

"I'd better not have another. I've child support to pay you know."

"Child support?" would come back as a query. The story of how he'd fathered a child to a woman less than half his age would be reluctantly drawn out of him. He got the story, with all its hesitations, down to a fine art.

Henry even went back to the pub where he had met Sharlene. He enquired about her as an introduction to telling his tale once more. The locals were stoic and told him she was long gone. Behind his back they wondered if Sharlene had really been pregnant when she left the village. If she had been, how could Henry be so sure he was the father given Sharlene had also been going out with a pharmacy rep. from Harrogate? That's who she had gone away with.

The final word on the matter came from Henry's third

wife. She'd heard the story from others who had been regaled with Henry's so called worries about money due to the child support he had to pay. She ran in to him by chance outside of the post office.

"I hear you put a tart in the pudding club," she said, "I'm pleased it wasn't me. Another one of you in the world would be two too many."

"Aye," was all Henry had to say.

"I also hear," said his ex-wife, "that you are paying her child support."

"Happen, I cannot tell a lie," Henry replied.

"I always thought you were a daft bugger but nowt as queer as this. You know as well as I do that you had the snip when we were first married."

Back in the village where he'd met Sharlene the locals would recall the story, from time to time, usually with the rejoinder,

"An old fool and his money." This was always added sotto voce.

Chapter Seven
The War Ace

Dave was dwelling on the strangeness of egos when he turned to walk past his old school. Looking at the old place now he felt grateful for the time he'd spent there, not so much for the buildings and certainly not for the traditions. He'd so often in life found traditions were used as control mechanisms by the unimaginative to supress initiative and advancement. The sense of warmness Dave had was for some of the teachers who had not only become mentors but also friends.

When attending the school he had been accused of being a regicidal maniac. He was told he was the prime suspect in a plot to throw acid on the Queen Mother when she was to attend the school's quatercentenary with it having been established during the reign of Elizabeth I. Dave told the police that not only was he innocent but he'd make it easy for them by refusing to attend the celebrations. A friend had equally wanted to opt out but was press ganged into playing a trumpet fanfare for the royal visitor. If he refused he would be committed to hell and damnation and could forget about being given a reference to get into university.

Dave shook his head in remembrance of such things. Some of the teachers were good, some bad, some indifferent and some just plain lazy. Some were outright thugs and some took sarcasm to a new height and delighted in berating someone or other for half the lesson or more. The best were the enthusiasts, people who had a passion for what they taught. Some were respected for what they had done before they came into teaching such as the former Second World War fighter pilot who had ended up with artificial legs after a crash.

This reminded Dave of Isaac, the Second World War fighter pilot he had met in New Zealand. He had volunteered as soon as he could as he wanted revenge but first of all he had to learn a new language.

He told how his family had been displaced more than once over the years but had settled down and built up a comfortable farm. They felt relatively secure and were happy. Then the occupying forces came, who seized the farm, rounded up the people who could only take the clothes they were wearing. They weren't allowed to take any personal possessions. As they were taken off they could see their farm buildings being burnt. The cattle and animals were slaughtered and the crops destroyed. The farm hands were taken away separately.

They were marched to a gathering point, a field surrounded by barbed wire. They had no shelter, given little to drink and even less to eat, no medical aid for the sick and infirm, nothing. There they were held for some days before being forced to march on. As they marched through the country the locals in the neighbourhood were encouraged to come and attack them. People were wounded and murdered but all they were told to do was to keep marching.

Eventually they ended up with others like them in a hastily constructed concentration camp. It was inadequate to house the number who were crammed in. They didn't even have a building to sleep in. They slept on the bare earth in tents. Food and water was rationed and if it was thought that they favoured the enemy then they received even less. The sanitation was almost non-existent. They asked for help but received none.

The overcrowding and primitive conditions soon led to disease breaking out, typhoid, measles and dysentery became rife. The medical care was hostile. One of the young girls taken into the medical building was dying from a combination of starvation and illness. This triggered compassion in one of the nurses who was told to ignore her, she was just making a fuss.

Largely the inmates were left to their own totally inadequate healthcare based on housewives' tales and whatever remedies could be got hold of. Isaac told Dave of the deaths from disease in the camps, the children and the old, succumbed bit by inevitable bit. He had heard stories of some being thrown out of the camp to fend for themselves but who never got very far. It wasn't just hundreds that died, thousands died, and the world turned a blind eye. Isaac could recite the names of those he had lost in his family.

It was this anger that found him behind the controls of a fighter plane. He would exact his revenge and he did his best against the enemy who had treated his family so callously. He was disappointed when he was transferred to another front, he would have preferred to stay fighting where he had been but orders were orders. That was the price he had to pay for joining the Luftwaffe.

He felt that lasting legacy of bitterness that was to be found amongst the Boers after the war with the British. Records hadn't been kept but he had seen estimates that up to 28,000 Boers had died in concentration camps, four out of five of them had been children. He knew of the suffering from the stories passed down in his own family. As for the farm hands who'd been taken away, the British did not bother to keep records for native Africans housed in camps, but he'd heard their death toll was as bad as that in any of the camps imprisoning the Boers.

Isaac said he felt disillusioned after the war was over to discover that Germany had been worse than the British with their use of concentration camps. If he'd known he would have made some different decisions but he wasn't sure that he could have brought himself to fight with the British, maybe, but probably not. He just didn't know, but he did know that people should never have to be treated the way they had been.

Chapter Eight
Family Secrets

In his musings Dave found he was wandering down Duke Street and was walking once again past the Town Clock. He wondered what the reaction would be if someone put a road beacon on the spire, maybe as muted as the time one of his contemporaries had placed a waste paper bin on the apex of his old school's roof.

Dave headed in the direction of where he used to live; down Tubwell Row and along Parkgate towards Yarm Road passing the Hippodrome Theatre, centre for the Northern Philharmonic and other, not so salubrious entertainments.

Dave recalled that he had once booked tickets at a theatre to go with his wife and see what he thought was a much acclaimed kitchen sink drama. It wasn't the first time he'd got titles of films and shows mixed up. They had gone to see Von Ryan's Express when he thought they were going to see Ryan's Daughter. He was aware on that occasion that something was wrong when Frank Sinatra popped up at the start instead of John Mills. Anyway, the much acclaimed musical that Dave thought he was going to see turned out to be Paul Raymond's Pyjama Tops instead of the Pyjama Game. The plot of this show was that at regular intervals young women would find the flimsiest of excuses to take off their clothes and jump into a glass fronted swimming pool on the stage.

Dave and his wife were talking to an usherette at half time and having a good laugh at the show. The usherette pointed to an older man who was an usher near the stage.

"See that daft old bugger," she said, "last week he was limping around as if death's door was just around the corner. Since this show's been on he's been dancing and flouncing around such that he'd put Nijinsky to shame."

As Dave walked past the Hippodrome and up the hill at Banktop he remembered having to paddle his first motor bike up it while slipping the clutch. It was a pre-second world war 98cc Excelsior. It was as gutless as a Whitby kipper. That motorbike may still be around somewhere as Dave had sold it to a collector.

Dave remembered upgrading to a BSA Bantam influenced by his mate John having one. But even with more power there were still hills that needed to be walked up. He had been a pillion on John's bike to Whitby. Coming back it was obvious the motor cycle wasn't going to carry both of them up Loftus Bank, so Dave had to take to Shank's pony.

John was a tall chap, well over the six foot mark. Dave

had once gone for a ride with John as his pillion. As he was overtaking a vehicle he got a tap on the shoulder and told to move out as John didn't want knee capping. He hadn't realised how far John's legs stuck out; they were like elephant's ears with the wind behind them, or even more like a taxi with the doors wide open.

Once Dave was well into his walk along Yarm Road he recalled where the allotments had once been where the family had tried to grow vegetables after his dad had died, an exercise more in hope than reality. Dave reflected on how families could be both close and loving yet on the other hand still have their secrets.

He had been visiting Joan, one of his relatives, who had been a widow for many a year. As ever the conversation, over a cup of tea, covered familiar ground, the current deplorable state of politics and politicians, they were all as crooked as a corkscrew; the crappy weather, it was always either too hot or too cold but never like the little bear's bowl of porridge, just right. After the latest front page scandal, expressed in two inch high print on the front of the tabloid press, came the retelling of family shenanigans and petty scandals of one sort or the other. There was the cousin who liked men in uniform, especially bus conductors, that had to be chortled over one more time. Dave was politely nodding and only half paying attention when the conversation went off piste.

"How do you find somebody?"

"Sorry?" responded Dave as he changed to some form of alertness from semi-somnolence.

"How do you find somebody? I asked my son Wilf but he couldn't be bothered. How do you find somebody?"

"Tell me more, who are you looking for?" enquired Dave.

"I was wondering what happened to Dai Jones."

"Dai Jones," repeated Dave, "and where did he hail from?"

"From Wales," replied Joan.

" Dai Jones from Wales. Well that will eliminate half the men in Wales from any enquiry as a starter," said Dave with a touch of cynicism.

"I was just wondering," persisted Joan, "I thought you might be able to help seeing as you know about computers and things."

"I'll see what I can do, but can you give me any more information to help like whereabouts in Wales he might be from."

"Tenby, I was a waitress in Tenby just before the war, that's where I met him."

"An old boyfriend?" quizzed Dave.

"He might have been. None of your business," replied Joan rather abruptly.

"What would your Tommy think?" asked Dave pulling her leg by referring to Joan's long dead husband. Joan ignored the question and huffily said,

"Well, if you don't want to help then don't." Suitably chastised Dave promised to see what he could do.

"I'll tell you what I find next time I call," promised Dave.

A couple of weeks went by before Dave called on Joan again. There was much more bustle about her than usual as she prepared the cup of tea, it bordered on an anticipated excitement. There was no fore-chat about politicians, doolally relatives; there was nothing. The moment she had eased herself into her favourite chair, she started,

"Well?"

"Pleased to see you too," teased Dave, "Well what?"

"Well, did you track him down?"

"Sorry to tell you that so far I've found no sign of him.

Given it's Wales I would have expected to have found any number of Dai Jones in the phone book but do you know how many there are in Tenby?"

"A few I would have thought," answered Joan.

"Well so far I've found exactly none."

"None?" Joan shrugged her shoulders in disappointment.

"He must have meant a lot to you, was he your first boyfriend?"

"First serious boyfriend. He was lovely. He used to come and pick me up on his motorbike when I wasn't working. I say, 'his motorbike,' he used to borrow it from a friend. He couldn't afford a motorbike as he didn't have much money as he had no job. I was as poor as a church mouse, as I had nothing much left after paying my board. Between me and the pocket money he made from doing odd jobs, we had sufficient to put some petrol in the tank. We explored the countryside and beaches around Tenby. It was lovely countryside."

"I hadn't realised, until we spoke the last time we met, that you'd been to Wales. What took you there?" asked Dave.

"I just wanted to get away from home. There were ten of us in a two bedroomed cottage and being one of the older ones I was forever mothering the youngsters, there was no time for myself. I answered an advert for a job as a waitress that was in the classified ads of a magazine. I think I was given the job as they reckoned that given my family background I must know how to work hard. I couldn't wait to get away."

"How did you meet Dai?" enquired Dave.

"I first met him at a dance in the local chapel hall. We hit it off right away. It helped that he was both handsome and funny. He had worked on one of the local fishing boats but lost his job when the skipper had to take on one of his relatives who'd lost his job elsewhere. That's how it was in those days. Anyway, he swept me off my feet and would turn up whenever we could get together. Sometimes, we'd just go for a walk and sometimes he'd turn up wearing leather trousers which meant the motor bike was propped up just around the corner." Joan smiled with the memory of it all.

"So that's why you get excited when we are out in the car and we are overtaken by a motorcyclist crouched over their tank wriggling their taught leather cheeks at you?" Dave said taking the mickey.

"I don't know what you are talking about," said Joan with a larger than usual smile.

"There are a couple of more areas I can have a look for your Mr Jones. I'll let you know how I get on the next time we catch up," said Dave on parting.

He now had some understanding of why Joan's son, Wilf, had not wanted to help his mother. He thought he'd have to be careful he didn't walk into a family minefield.

The next time Dave called on Joan she was a little more muted on his arrival. A cup of tea as usual was offered and accepted. Dave apologised to Joan and told her he'd been busy with work and hadn't had a chance to make any further enquiries but he'd get back to it as soon as he could.

He was more than a little hesitant before he ventured in to a conversation which he wasn't sure how it would go. He spoke more to the carpet in Joan's direction rather than looking her in the eye.

"Forgive me saying it Joan but I feel a little uncomfortable making these enquiries. I feel as if I'm maybe doing something your family would rather I didn't. Why are you looking for Dai Jones? It seems like a statement of regret for the life you had with Tommy."

Joan paused before replying, "It's true I've never told Wilf, or anyone else, anything about my time in Wales. It had its moments both good and at times, not so good. If things had been different I could well still be living there. Unfortunately, my mother was taken ill and I was asked to return home to look after her and the family."

Joan broke off to go looking for some biscuits, it was as if she needed a bit of time to think. When she settled back down in her chair she continued.

"Tommy lived just up the road from us and he began calling around. At last he started asking me to go out, a walk here, a dance in the church hall there. I still wasn't at all sure he was all that interested as we must have gone out half a dozen times before he first kissed me. By that time war had been declared but Tommy was rejected for the Services because he had flat feet. He spent the war at a factory making aircraft instruments. That meant he was around a lot and as I got to know him bit by bit; I started to like him."

Again Joan took a pause for reflection before suddenly bursting out, "You nosey old cow!" Dave was taken aback but noticed Joan was staring out of the window.

"What?" he enquired.

"That nosey old cow there," Joan nodded her head in the direction of a woman's back who was walking away from them on the opposite footpath of the street.

"I'll give her an endoscope next time to see if she can spot what I had for breakfast." Joan approached the window and scowled a bit more at the woman's back.

"Nosey old cow," she repeated somewhat softer before turning back into the room. "Now where was I? Yes, Tommy and I were married and were happy enough until his heart attack. He was a conservative chap; grey flannels and a sports coat were his living skin. He liked a pint with the lads on a Saturday night but never came home drunk. He was the scorer for the local cricket team which he'd supported all his life. All round he was a decent sort of fellow, he treated me well. I never once saw him without any clothes on. I tried to tempt him once in the bedroom by showing him some flesh but he told me to get something on quick before I caught my death. He was steady. We always went to a cottage in Reeth for our holidays. In the early days we'd get a train to Richmond then bike our way up the dale but later on we'd get a bus all the way. He didn't want to learn to drive or buy a car, he was happy as he was. We were happy enough until he died. I take flowers or a plant up to his grave each week. He deserves that."

Once again Joan paused even longer in thought and Dave took the opportunity to excuse himself. He promised to see if there was anything further he could do to track down Dai Jones, and said he would call again soon.

The next time Dave called on Joan she seemed more subdued. After the obligatory tea was served they settled down and it wasn't long before Joan asked if Dave had got anywhere.

"I'm afraid not," replied Dave, "I've tried searching the records for council rates and online census documents, sorry, but I can't find him anywhere."

"Well he's maybe dead by now," said Joan rather gloomily.

"So, what happened to you and our mysterious Mr Jones?" asked Dave.

"As you know I came home to look after the family when my mother was taken ill. At the same time Dai found a job on a tramp steamer sailing out of Liverpool. I wrote for a while care of the ship owner's office in Liverpool. I don't know if my letters were ever passed on. Occasionally, I'd receive a letter or a postcard from Timbuctoo or wherever his ship was docked, he never acknowledged my letters to him. I became so busy looking after the family that in time I just stopped writing and about the same time his postcards dried up. Maybe he didn't even survive the war; a lot of merchant seamen were lost."

"Sorry, I couldn't help you find Dai," apologised Dave again.

"It would have been nice to know what happened to Dai but it wasn't so much him. It was our son. It would have been nice to know that he'd had a good life."

"Your son?" asked Dave in surprise.

"Yes, we had a son but couldn't afford to keep him. He was adopted by one of Dai's relatives but I wasn't allowed to know who. That was the times we lived in I suppose. I thought if I could have found Dai I could have found out what happened to him. It would have been nice to know."

"Does your Wilf know about this?" asked Dave.

"No, and that's the way I want it to stay."

Chapter Nine
Ghost Story

Dave decided to take a side trip down Eastbourne Road. This was a road his mother inveigled him to take on his way home from junior school when the more usual track through the allotments was muddy; sometimes he did and sometimes he didn't. Sometimes he got into trouble and sometimes he didn't. He'd learned to read his mother's deep sigh as to which way it would go.

Dave looked for the house that had a pointed roof porch as its entrance. It was one in a row of terraced houses. For reasons he could no longer recall it was known as the 'witch's' house.

Did an old woman with warts on her nose once live there? What Dave could recall was the compulsion to run past it, on the other side of the road, and as quickly as possible. When he was a house away from where the 'witch' lived he would stop, get on his starting blocks by lining up on a crack in the pavement and then run as if the hounds of Hell were on his tail. He would only stop when he was well clear of the 'witch's' house and out of breath. If nothing else it made sure he arrived home sooner than he might otherwise have done. Sadly, as Dave walked along he could no longer recognise the house.

The thought of witches and the supernatural made him think of the ability to commune with those from another world.

Some thought his grandfather had the gift. He could be sitting in front of the miner's ever present fire in his two up and two down cottage when the temperature in the room would suddenly drop to a shivering cold. He would point with his finger a little to the left of the door from the scullery.

"There he is, he's there," he'd proclaim, but to others in the room there was nothing to see.

There was a tale of a miner in his coffin who suddenly rose up and pointed from beneath his shroud to one of the women mourners. The next day her husband was killed in a roof fall down the pit. The other world was not to be trifled with.

His grandmother had worked as a servant in a large hall near Brusselton Folly and from time to time she also had to go to the Folly to carry out her duties. She told tales of a room in the hall that was locked after the death of its occupant in mysterious circumstances. Everybody was forbidden to enter. After night fall the servants didn't like having to pass near this room even holding their best trimmed candle. There were stories of mysterious knockings and, from time to time, sightings of an apparition, a woman in grey, passing through the walls.

Dave's mother had told him that she first experienced the other world when she was a young girl living in the miner's cottage where her father used to see what others didn't. She was asleep in her bed and she felt something moving over her legs. She'd screamed and her father came rushing in. Her room was searched but there was nothing to be found. Her father proclaimed that it must have been a spectre.

Dave pointed out to his mother that there was no electricity upstairs in that cottage. To get some light on to the subject you had to find the box of matches in the dark, and then light the tilly lamp, having taken time to get out of bed. None of this would have been instantaneous, and it could well have been just a common or garden rattus rattus that had run over her legs. He told her that he had no doubt that if the rat had any self-respect then it would have disappeared down the way it had come long before any tilly lamp was lit. All his mother would say, in a very knowing manner, was that she knew what she'd experienced and it wasn't a rat. Dave's subsequent question of, 'a mouse?' got a look that would have shrivelled the finest piece of chamois into a scrotum.

Dave's mother used to regularly visit her sister who had married a shepherd. They lived in a small Yorkshire village in a house that had, pre-Henry VIII, been part of Jervaulx Abbey's estate. In the ceiling of the main living room was what was described as the most perfect cross. The house had its priest hole camouflaged near the chimney breast. Water was obtained from a hand pump across the yard at the rear of the house. It was while fetching some water that Dave's mother told him that she'd seen the apparition of a headless monk. It was walking across the yard heading towards the water pump. As it drew near to the well it disappeared. She said she'd only seen it the once but she said she knew it was there. Dave had noted that his mother was known to succumb very easily to a drop of parsnip wine.

Dave's brother, Ned, believed he'd inherited his mother's sixth sense and had a prescience to know that things would happen before they actually happened particularly when it came to matters of the family.

One evening Dave and Ned had been out for a drink with their respective girlfriends and a few others. After the pubs had closed they all went back the flat of Ned's girlfriend which she shared with another girl. They lived in one of those big but non-descript houses, set in a large garden, which could have been anything from late Georgian to Edwardian. At that point in time such houses had fallen out of favour and were being carved up into flats for students and young people.

On this particular night there was the usual after pub banter and bonhomie taking place. The general conversations covered everything in the universe and well beyond. In the course of the discussion it emerged there was hearsay that the house they were in was haunted. Ned immediately became interested. He put on his most serious all-knowing look and said that they should try and communicate with the ghost. There was a murmuring of general agreement. A large piece of cardboard was produced along with a tumbler which was soon turned into a ouija board by writing out the alphabet and the numbers 0 to 9 in a circle broken by two boxes, one saying 'yes' and one saying 'no'. The tumbler was placed upside down in the centre of the circle and everyone was implored to put a finger on it. The scene was set for the portents to be revealed and for the secrets of the ghost to be uncovered.

"Is anybody there?" intoned Ned in his most sepulchral manner. The tumbler whizzed to the 'yes' box.

"Who are you?" continued Ned in a commanding voice. The tumbler started to spell out, a-u-n-t, before pausing for a rest, then continued, s-h-e-i-l-a. One of the girls gave a gasp,

"Aunt Sheila," she said. "Is that you?" The tumbler made its way to the 'yes' box.

Before anything further happened a discussion started about whether one or another of the participants was actually pushing the tumbler around. All protested their innocence and Ned proclaimed that it must be the spirits from the other side that was moving it. He recommenced the session by asking,

"Aunt Sheila, are you still there?" The tumbler moved to the 'yes' box once more. It was elicited from Aunt Sheila that the young person in question was going to get married, have 2 children and live a happy life.

Aunt Sheila was replaced by Uncle Edward who had special interest for one person then Cousin Gertrude for another. After which Ned said it was time to become serious and talk with the ghost of the house. The temperature of the room dropped a couple of degrees before Ned had gained the attention of everyone and then intoned,

"Is the ghost of the house present?" There was complete silence.

"I know you are here; I can feel your presence," said Ned.

"Is the ghost of the house present?" repeated Ned. Again there was silence.

"I know it is here, I just know it," continued Ned addressing all in the room.

"Is the ghost of the house present?" was repeated for a third time. The tumbler flew across the ouija board passing the 'no' enroute to landing in someone's lap.

"I knew it," said Ned in triumph and totally ignored the contradiction of the 'no' answer.

"What we need to do is to go and meet the ghost on their territory. Who's going to join me outside on the landing?" A couple of chaps staunchly agreed they needed to join Ned to help rid the girl's flat of any threats posed by phantoms. The girls needn't be afraid, they were there to look after them. Dave revealed his lack of staunchness and stayed where he was. He continued to be engaged with the remaining members of the group gathered around the ouija board. After a couple of more rounds of interrogating guardian angels about the marital futures and well-being of those present, it was then that Uncle Erasmus turned up looking for David. Dave learnt that his guardian angel would keep a look out for him and that he'd end up happily married with two children. Dave protested that he didn't have an Uncle Erasmus but the believers in the room said he must have, maybe he was just a bit removed.

Dave and his girlfriend decided it was time to leave. Dave muttered to himself that Uncle Erasmus was so far removed he must be from Mars. Anyway, no Uncle Erasmus had featured on any family tree that he had ever researched. Dave had a sense that there was nothing like a bad spirit to spoil a good party.

At this point Ned tells the story and said he and his friends had left the room to commune with the ghost. After a while they had made contact. It turned out the ghost was a woman, dressed in blue, who was married for her money and once married had been locked up in the basement and slowly starved to death. Ned said he was just about to ask the spectre what needed to be done to help alleviate her distress when all of a sudden the door to the lounge was suddenly flung open. This was immediately followed by a blue flash and a large explosion and he and his pals were thrown against the wall.

Dave will tell you he had said goodnight to everyone in the lounge and then opened the door to leave. He said goodnight to his brother and his mates, who were sat around in a circle on the floor looking very earnest, and went home with his girlfriend.

Dave also denies having had undue influence on the tumbler that flew across the room that had landed in someone's lap. After all he'd only meant it to stop on 'no', which he thought would have been quite funny, but he recognised he could be a little bit gauche at times. Dave also wondered if his brother had a secret penchant for parsnip wine.

Chapter Ten

Web of Deceit

As Dave walked on to Cobden Street he recognised a house where Jonty used to live. Jonty was often detached like the house. Dave didn't know Jonty all that well as he was much younger than him but he was, from everything Dave had heard, a geek with a heart of gold. Dave had been impressed with Jonty's capabilities and his underlying sense of fun but was equally aware that not all shared this view of him with the result that he had been bullied.

His parents were that rare breed of all round nice people. They were regular church goers with a liberal perspective. They saw good in just about everyone and had a great sense of right and wrong. This morality passed down to Jonty by more than just osmosis and if anything, it was reinforced by the bullying he had suffered from time to time. He couldn't understand why anyone would take exception to him moving a worm, that was crawling across a pavement, to the safety of a garden, but he knew to his cost that that could excite venom and derision.

There was another lad, Colin, who lived in Cobden Street not too far away from Jonty. He was one who would give Jonty a bit of a hard time whenever he could. Colin had been given a rarity in those days, a radio controlled car that he proudly drove up and down the street, whilst threatening life changing injuries to anyone who came near it. Jonty sensed some fun could be had at Colin's expense. He researched radio control mechanisms before buying some components and making one for himself. The device had to be tuneable to find the right wave length and had to be powerful enough to override the other lad's remote control. There was some experimentation and it was a bit hit and miss before Jonty found the right formula.

After that Jonty had fun hiding behind the curtains in his bedroom and having Colin's car turn right when the lad was trying to make it turn left. Colin was mystified when the car seemed to have a mind of its own. He'd pick it up, examine it, shake it and be pleased when all seemed well again. Then there were times when he went to pick the car up and it ran away from him down the street with Colin in quick pursuit. It could then suddenly stop with him having to do a skip and a jump to prevent himself from standing on it. The car lost a bit of paint and suffered a couple of dents after running into walls and gutters but, all in all, it was enjoyed both by Colin and Jonty.

Colin shouldn't have bullied Jonty that day, if he hadn't, then both he and Jonty might have enjoyed the car for many more months. As it was Colin decided to purposely bump into Jonty in the street and accuse Jonty of bumping into him, before despatching him a 'dead leg', a knee despatched to the upper part of the leg which was very painful. Jonty didn't say much but his sense of fairness was offended. He waited until Colin had his car in the street again. He had a sense of satisfaction as the remote controlled car ran up and down the road giving Colin a good run around for his money. Jonty maybe got carried away a little as he reeked his revenge to the extent that he accidently flipped his controls the wrong way and the car disappeared underneath the wheels of a coal lorry. It had been great fun whilst it lasted and he was sorry it was all over. Jonty then wondered what he could now build with the components of his remote control as it had no longer had a purpose.

Jonty was known to stand up for others when he thought there was an injustice but he could also stand up for himself even if it wasn't always obvious. Jonty learnt to play the guitar and learn it he did. He was a wizard and could play songs from the hit parade with very little trouble. He developed a bit of a following, he was respected for who he was and that meant he developed an immunity to anyone who thought they could be disparaging about him. He became both a tutor and one of the youngest examiners in guitar but to him, it was a hobby, a joy and a pastime.

Jonty's interest lay in electronics, gadgets and all things digital. He completed a degree in Computer Science but found it hard going as he thought some of the tutors were not keeping up with the advancements of the digital age. Through gaming he found his way into the dark web. This was an ever changing universe of anonymous people, groupings, organisations and governments who were exploiting the digital world for their own ends. It was an anarchic world quite frequently not being used for the good and was easily twice as big as the internet.

One of the good things coming out of the computer course was that he met Lilian. They fell in love over gaming and code writing; programs and apps were their shared passion and joy. They also had the same ethical outlook and from time to time would work to track down and thwart scammers. It wasn't always easy as unsurprisingly, the person being scammed didn't always believe that they were being defrauded.

Jonty had managed to listen in to a scammer persuading a pensioner that his bank account had been compromised by the people working in the bank's branch. The scammer persuaded the pensioner that in order to safeguard his money he needed to withdraw it, parcel it up and post it to a safe address. If asked by the people serving behind the counter at the Post Office what the parcel contained the pensioner was tutored to tell them that it contained documents.

After the call was over, Jonty phoned the pensioner to warn him that what he was being asked to do was a scam and warned him not to do it. As soon as he'd put the phone down Jonty detected the pensioner contacting the scammer to tell him what had happened. The scammer told the pensioner that he'd been contacted by a corrupt bank official and that he should continue to get his money and post it to the address he'd been given, as soon as possible, before he lost it.

Unfortunately, Jonty didn't know the pensioner's bank so did the next best thing. He tracked down the nearest Post Office to the pensioner's home and alerted them to the package the pensioner was going to send. They were reluctant to become involved as once they'd received a parcel it was their duty to deliver it. They did, however, agree to contact the police so that the package could be intercepted. The police then took action from there as they now had the address of a money mule that they could investigate. Jonty was pleased with the result but shook his head at the way some people just couldn't be saved from themselves.

After getting their degrees Jonty and Lilian married. He pursued a career in digital security whilst Lilian worked in the gaming industry. Jonty had joined a large firm of consultants where his technical knowledge and knowhow quickly advanced him up the ladder and he became a partner at a comparatively young age. He was fortunate that his expertise meant that clients sought him out, rather than Jonty having to suffer the fate of some of his fellow partners. They had to work very hard keeping the work flowing in and meeting their targets which were ultimately set by the New York head office. Jonty knew he wasn't suited to the 'hail and well met' world that his fellow partners endured and was thankful for his lot.

Jonty first met Cindy when she was assigned to him as his personal assistant. She was both charming and efficient as well as being pretty. She relieved Jonty of the administrative burdens which he found a bore and a distraction from his interests in the fascinating digital world that he inhabited. Cindy was a great hit with him and made his life so much easier. As time went on she could anticipate more and more of his needs, some of which he hadn't even thought about.

Whilst a hit with Jonty, Cindy wasn't such a hit with her co-workers. They found her brash and aloof. She was ambitious and showed no signs of having concerns for others. Her sunshine smile was switched on when entering Jonty's office and just as easily switched off the moment she walked out. To those who cared to listen she declared she was going to marry Jonty one day. She was oblivious to being told that he was already married, 'that', she said, 'she already knew, so what?'

Jonty's sense of fairness was often offended in situations he encountered in the work he did. People, criminal organisations even government agencies hid in the anonymity of the digital world. Money was laundered and thefts committed on a grand scale involving both currencies and intellectual properties. Worst of all Jonty could see where people were being exploited and sold, slavery was alive and kicking. Even where it was possible to start to identify the people behind the anonymity, it was often impossible to get justice as governments and corrupt officials turned a blind eye and counted their ill-gotten gains for doing so. Justice could be illusionary. Hypocrisy stalked the highways and byways of the dark web. One of the largest complexity of servers which the criminal world used had been created by the U.S. Navy to hide the identity of their field agents.

Jonty was driven to helping people and organisations to avoid having their computer systems hacked and held to ransom or having their information stolen. Occasionally, he could trace the malefactors to somebody operating locally rather than in Ukraine, Russia or some other country where it was impossible to obtain justice. When this happened, in his early days, he had referred these cases to the national security agency that handled such things. The results were often disappointing, as the agency tramped around in their proverbial big boots. The hackers picked up the signs and disappeared with their ill-gotten gains back into digital anonymity, usually never to be identified again. It was a rare thing for such cases to come to court and when they did, both judges and juries had difficulty understanding the technology and complexities of the digital world and so those charged, too often, walked free.

Later on Jonty would refer such cases to Stan, Dan and Dan2, the junior of the trio. Dan2, who had red hair, was often referred to as the Fiery Inferno as Dante was seen as being a wonderful homonym for Dan2. Jonty had stumbled across these policemen by chance when they'd been working with a company where it was suspected one of the employees was operating a credit card scam on the side. Just one name and one identifiable account led to a lot of what Stan called 'good old fashioned police work'. This had resulted in the successful apprehension and prosecution of the suspect although it had been a close run call. The key witness had been on holiday totally unaware of the police's interest in him and his defrauded account. He returned just before a crucial deadline that the police had to meet in order for them to file their case.

Following this case Jonty and the three policemen became firm friends and would catch up for a drink most Thursday evenings. It had to be something truly extraordinary for Cindy to put anything other than this meeting into Jonty's diary. As the first glass of beer massaged their vocal cords they discussed the weather, sporting triumphs and travesties and any other trivia that came to mind. As the friendship developed all this became interjected with a banter of personal insults that seemed to know no bounds, much to their amusement.

By the second and third round of drinks the four of them were putting the world to rights. Invariably, the conversation always seemed to get around to the cops' experiences of criminals evading justice by telling lies, having friends and family lie or by using to their own advantage the constraints the cops had to work within. In some cases they knew the people funding and organising the thefts, the supply of drugs and so forth. Because the suspects never got their hands dirty themselves, the cops were unable to prove that the man with big house and garage with several expensive cars in it was a criminal. Any number of business activities were happily used to launder the proceeds. Apart from which, happily socialising with and hosting significant members of society, including senior police officers, never seemed to go amiss. In the beginning, Jonty didn't realise he knew the person living in the big house that the police were referring to.

The four frequently agreed that the law and justice did not always sleep in the same bed. Their sense of injustice was heightened more and more from what they could see was happening on the dark web with impunity. Stan's and the Dans' expertise in this area had grown exponentially under Jonty's tutelage.

Life may have gone on like this for some time with the world being a much better place every Friday morning but then, as the world will, things changed. The change had come about slowly. For some reason Lilian had started to withdraw from Jonty. He had to go away, from time to time, because of his job. He noticed when he returned home that Lilian's reception started to get colder and colder. Along with this she started to accuse him of having an affair. She wouldn't discuss it with him and just told him, she knew. Jonty's denials had no impact on her. Her behaviour started to become erratic and she had mood swings that alarmed Jonty. She became more and more withdrawn to the extent that she stopped going to her office. She told Jonty that she knew, people told her things. She wouldn't say what she'd been told or by whom. Jonty tried to get help for her but was frustrated by the mental health system. As Lilian wouldn't recognise that she needed help and because she hadn't harmed herself or anyone else then there was nothing that could be done for her. She'd turned her back on a private psychologist that Jonty had tried to introduce her to. Jonty became reluctant to go away with his job so that he could stay at home and support Lilian as best as he could unfortunately, that wasn't always possible.

Notwithstanding, when it happened, it came as a surprise. Jonty couldn't comprehend it. Prior to him leaving home

Lilian had seemed in a much better state than she had been for a while. She even saw him to the door, smiled and gave him a kiss. She was a bit more like her old self. He was feeling good as he took off to anonymously attend a hackers' conference in Kiev; this was at a time when the Russians didn't seem to be a threat. All was well with the world. Then the telephone call came summoning him back. Lilian had committed suicide. She'd jumped off a cliff. Jonty was devastated. A brief note was found, posted through the letterbox at home. It contained some incomprehensible ramblings in a script that could hardly be seen as hers ending in an apology to Jonty and her signature which was more recognisable.

Jonty went over everything in his own mind feeling guilty about not having done more for her. 'If only,' was the start to many of his thoughts. The experts brought little consolation and Jonty had to understand that their hands were tied when he'd tried to get her some help. 'You shouldn't blame yourself,' he was told.

Cindy said that Lilian had phoned her up and asked to meet her for a coffee on the day she had died. She said that when they met Lilian was in a distressed state with tears running down her face. Lilian had wanted assurance about Jonty's business trip. She said she believed that Jonty no longer loved her and he was having an affair. Cindy said she had reassured Lilian that as far as she knew and as far as office gossip went there was nothing to suggest Jonty was being unfaithful to her. Cindy said that over time Lilian had calmed down and seemed to have accepted what she had to say, she had thanked Cindy and told her she was going home. Cindy said she blamed herself for not doing more to help her, she thought Lilian was alright when she left her. She apologised over and over again to Jonty for not doing more. She said that if she had known Lilian was in that frame of mind then she would have done something about it but... Cindy left the sentence unfinished. Jonty and Cindy comforted each other.

The tragedy hung over them both through the post-mortem and the inquest. While prolonging the agony neither shed any new light on Lilian's death. For Jonty the biggest unexplained piece in the puzzle was the note which clearly wasn't in Lilian's normal handwriting other than the signature and why was it posted through the letterbox? It was incomprehensible. The experts were ambivalent on the issue saying anything was possible given Lilian's state of mind.

Jonty became lost in his work as his means of dealing with his sadness. Cindy became more and more crucial to him in making sure everything around him ran as smoothly as clockwork. She was more indispensable to him than ever. Any attempts by his work colleagues, other than by his fellow partners, to offer more than condolences were deflected by Cindy. This was particularly true with her fellow personal assistants where such attempts were rebutted with such fierce gusto that they learnt to keep well away.

Over time Thursday nights slowly lost their sombreness and gained something of their old gusto. Life turned back to being more of a norm. As it did so, Jonty's and Cindy's closeness led to romance and marriage. Cindy's fellow workers whispered behind her back in a mixture of awe and contempt,

"Well she said she'd get her man ..."

As Cindy became more and more embedded in Jonty's life she took over control of not only his business life but his private life as well. Jonty was happy for this to happen, it allowed him to concentrate on his work in an environment which was both complex and ever changing. Cindy's control extended to looking after Jonty's finances in which she took a particularly keen interest. In time, she persuaded Jonty to buy a house which had extensive grounds and a self-contained flat, which originally Cindy told him would be good for visitors. Before very long Cindy's parents had moved in when he was working away. They'd had a bit of a hard time and Cindy's father had made some poor business decisions. Cindy was sure that Jonty would understand that they preferred to do their own thing and be independent but they were good company for Cindy when Jonty wasn't there because of work. Cindy just knew Jonty would understand. The question of Cindy's parents paying some form of rent for the flat was never raised and they never offered. They were family and Cindy was quite happy for them to help themselves to the contents of her fridge and larder.

From time to time Jonty noticed Cindy and her parents whispering to each other and looking in his direction. If he didn't know better he would have thought they were conspiring but he put it down to a trait of that particular family's closeness, albeit he did think it verged on rudeness. Once, when he raised the issue with Cindy she dismissed it out of hand and told him he was talking nonsense.

After they had moved into the new house life reached a level of contentment. Jonty enjoyed his work with a lot of the humdrum of life deflected from him by Cindy. Thursday nights continued to be his boy's night out where it was reinforced time and again that victims were not always the recipients of justice. In Jonty's work he tried, where he could, to bring some sort of retribution to the wrongdoers but far too often they hid behind the cloaks of corruption and the dark web anonymity. This offended Jonty's sense of fairness.

It seemed that the routine of life that had been established could have gone on forever with contentment all around. The trigger for change came when Jonty discovered a jotter pad in Cindy's office at work where it looked as if she had been practising Jonty's signature. He queried why she was doing this,

"Just doodling" was her reply. A passing PA who overheard the conversation noted off hand,

"Just like you used to do with Lilian's signature." Cindy abruptly denied this.

In his working life Jonty had the need to exercise what he called professional scepticism. In his personal life he trusted people; more so for those who were close to him. He'd never needed to cross this divide by bringing the clinical analytics of his business life into his home life but the discovery of the doodles now challenged that.

Jonty had trouble with thinking what he was thinking but the thoughts weren't going away, his professional scepticism antennae had been aroused. He had a sense that his trust had been betrayed. Once he had convinced himself that he wasn't being stupid he started to become more alert.

His suspicions reached new heights when he heard a phone ringing in Cindy's wardrobe. Cindy was downstairs having a cup of tea with her parents so he went to look for the phone to answer it. The surprise was that it wasn't Cindy's regular phone as that was on her bedside table without a peep coming from it. After the phone had stopped ringing Jonty decided that he'd take a risk and download some software onto the phone that would allow him to interrogate it in his own good time. He listened for Cindy coming back up the stairs but was relieved that she was taking her time over her cup of tea. Thankfully, all was done and the phone safely back in its location before Cindy returned. Jonty thought his luck was in as she must have forgotten to turn the phone off when she last used it.

The phone that Jonty started to interrogate was an older model that had obviously been set up in a way to try and disguise the owner's identity. There were some financial transactions that obviously required closer scrutiny but that could wait. There was one thing that shocked him more than anything, there were messages to Lilian insinuating or claiming Jonty was being unfaithful to her. One of the last was an insidious message wondering what Jonty was getting up to on his trip to Kiev and raising the question about whether Jonty really was going to the Ukraine.

Jonty thought he needed a little more time to take this in and look more closely at what might have been going on. He was trying to pretend things were normal with Cindy but he couldn't help himself being cooler and avoiding her where he thought he could reasonably get away with it.

Cindy wasn't stupid and recognised that something was amiss. A couple of days later she arranged for them to have lunch together at a restaurant renowned for its food and service. She arrived a little late and joined Jonty at the table. She sat down in a matter of fact impersonal way. They ate their lunch with a glass of wine and made small talk much as if it was a meeting of strangers. At the end of the meal, when they were having a coffee, Cindy told Jonty she was leaving him.

"By the way," she went on to tell him, "The house is mine so please move out, find yourself a hotel tonight."

Jonty knew he shouldn't have been surprised but couldn't but help being tongue tied. Things had come to a head much sooner than he'd expected. While Cindy had the advantage she went on to tell him that his invested funds were also in her name. By necessity Jonty had to follow Cindy out of the restaurant as he'd been left with the bill to pay. He caught sight of her driving away in a brand new European sports car.

Jonty's inward anger was still with him when he retired to a hotel with a few clothes and his laptop. Following the discovery of Cindy's hidden phone he'd had the fortitude to also instal some spyware on her usual phone. There was much that he needed to know.

It is said you can hack into anything that has a chip in it no matter how secure. A hacker had once gained access to a company's secrets through its aquarium. The heat and oxygen monitor was linked to a manager's cell phone and voilà as they say in France. It is also known that a car's systems can easily be hacked into via the driver's cell phone. Some speculated that Jonty would have been able to do this and be able to cover up any trace. Be that as it may, it is a matter of record that the following day Cindy was behind the wheel of her new car when it drove off the road when speeding excessively. Sadly for her parents, Cindy died at the scene.

Later forensic examination of the car's chips and electronic records confirmed she'd been driving far too fast and there was no evidence to the contrary. Obviously, she was a driver who was inexperienced with such a powerful sportscar that was new to her.

Following the crash, Jonty found that luck favoured him. Cindy hadn't changed her will from the days when she and Jonty had married and vowed to leave everything to each other in the event of their demise. It seemed fair that everything should revert to him. He wasn't particularly malicious but found he had more joy than he felt he should have when he put his house up for sale. It was just justice for his former in-laws. He felt they had encouraged their daughter down the path she had taken. Now, their wish had come true, they could have the independence they said they wanted when they had initially moved into the flat.

∞

Jonty was unsettled by everything that had gone on, he felt himself all over the place, he could end up feeling both ends of the spectrum of any one emotion almost simultaneously. He took a break before returning to his roll at the consultancy firm but, whereas before he had trusted people to do things for him, he now tended to oversee everything and in detail. He still did his job very competently but the vigour and verve of his former years was missing.

The uncertainty he felt meant he rented an apartment rather than put a stake in the ground again by buying another house. He reverted to driving an older classic car, something that was truly mechanical and didn't need a computer to diagnose any ills. In other words he had a car he knew wasn't hackable and was fun to drive albeit with not quite the safety rating of a newer car.

Thursday nights became more than ever the highlight of his week with the four of them sometimes enjoying indiscrete conversations. But for the four of them, Stan, Dan, the Fiery Inferno and Jonty, it was Chatham House rules, where nothing discussed was ever going to be repeated anywhere else.

One of their sessions covered the frustrations of seeing a dealer being given a very light sentence when he had sold considerable quantities of goods stolen from lorries. They knew that with remission he'd be out on the street again before he'd hardly been inside. They also knew he'd be wiser than he was the last time. It was just a variation on sending young offenders to a boot camp. When they come out they are fitter than when they went in and therefore became harder to catch.

The conversation led to a discussion as to what is a perfect crime. There was immediate agreement that it was a crime you got away with, but just as quickly they all realised that there was more to it than that. The Fiery Inferno asked if it was a perfect crime where a criminal traffics people on the dark web and is able to profit from it through the use of digital currency. All of this whilst hiding behind the anonymity that the dark web provided as well as living in a country that turned a blind eye to such activities. All agreed that such a crime might be something that the criminals could get away with but their actions were despicable and far from perfect.

The four of them then moved on to discuss the political environment, some recent scientific research, and ended up with Stan and Dan becoming very excited about the physics of super yachts and the design of sails that maximised the different behaviour of wind over the sea. Jonty observed that he'd heard that watching grass grow could become very exhilarating. Dan said he didn't understand. Dan2 explained, that he didn't wish to take the wind out of Stan's and Dan's sails but if they hadn't noticed, Jonty wasn't into yachting. A hint was taken and the conversation moved on.

The following Thursday the four met and after talking about the latest litany of injustices they discussed whether such failures justified vigilantes. Stan and both the Dans immediately asserted that nothing justified vigilantes. All could attest to examples where ill-informed people had tried to take justice into their own hands and had meted out a greater injustice. Unfortunately, it was the loners, the eccentrics and the oddballs that inevitably became victims of such action. Being both judge and jury was sure to court disaster.

Jonty probed this a bit further. He asked them to imagine an environment not too dissimilar to the Wild West in the United States in the nineteenth century where the law could be absent or transient at its best. He wondered if there was a case for vigilantes if they were based on a shared moral code connected to a forensic approach to investigating crime. He wondered if that was a counter to the criminals who operated with their own code which aimed at helping them with their criminal activities and avoiding detection.

There was a begrudging acceptance that in the absence of anything then vigilantes may well be better than nothing, providing they were based on standards. Jonty left this thought to mature in the minds of the other three. He moved the conversation onto a lighter theme.

"Let's assume," he asked, "that we committed the perfect crime and had sufficient funds to live wherever we liked, where would that be?" The four's fantasies took them around the globe based on holidays they'd had and holidays they would like to have. Jonty then limited their choices by suggesting the need for reasonable civilised infrastructures and political stability. This ruled out South Sea Island paradises, more so when it was suggested that the idyl could be quickly destroyed by rustling the undergrowth. Spain was ruled out because too many criminals had gone to live there already.

Stan wondered what was wrong with where they lived. Dan thought it fine in summer but wouldn't it be nice to live somewhere warmer in winter, Australia sounded like a good idea.

The following Thursday Jonty invited the three around to his apartment for a curry rather than meeting in the pub. After they had eaten, they sat around drinking a glass of beer as Jonty entertained them on his guitar. As he played he started the conversation by suggesting the perfect crime might be to scam the scammers. Not the people who had robbed banks, as the banks should be big enough to look after themselves but maybe the others where there were many victims but where it would be difficult to directly recompense them for their loss. Or maybe where it was impossible to identify the original victims because the head of the crime syndicate was able to keep a distance and anonymity from the crimes they were having committed through a string of minions.

Dan agreed that if it was possible to make crime less lucrative then maybe there might be less of it. He also pointed out that life was comparatively cheap on the dark web and that it was too easy to hire an assassin. If anybody was to involve themselves in such an activity then they'd have to be immaculate about ensuring their own anonymity as the stakes would be high.

Stan said that if ever people such as themselves entered into this type of activity then they'd have to have their own code of silence and make sure they never discussed what they were doing either on-line or in a public environment.

Dan2 added that they'd have to divide the work with, let's say, him and Stan doing the researching and scamming and, Jonty and Dan following their every step and searching the web to make sure there was no lapse of anonymity. They would be the quality assurance team.

Jonty pointed out that they'd no doubt end up with far more money in their coffers than they needed after covering their running and living costs. They'd need a contingency to meet the unknown but after that he was sure there would be plenty left over that they could donate to suitable charities. They would need to carefully pick the charities that would do something constructive for victims. Jonty noted that there were as many rogues in the Not-For-Profit field as anywhere else.

They all sat back with smiles on their faces at the very thought and agreed it would be a wonderful thing to be able to put the world to rights like that.

"And I know where I'd start," said Dan2, "that man with his big house and garage stuffed full with exotic cars."

"I suspect," said Jonty, "it wouldn't be too difficult to hack into his computer, most likely through his security system. All things are possible."

Once again they all settled back in their chairs supping on their beer agreeing that it would be really good to bring some kind of justice to bear. If only they could in their wildest dreams make it happen.

By the time autumn came around Jonty had recognised that he was never going to find job satisfaction at the consultancy firm again, consequently, much to the chagrin of the firm, he resigned his partnership. He agreed to undertake one-off assignments with them in the future if there was something juicy that tickled his interest. He then dropped out of sight.

∞

Jonty softly hummed to himself as he walked by the River Yarra in Melbourne on a fine Australian spring day. He was in his shirt sleeves and heading towards a restaurant. There was a lightness in his step that had been missing for a while. The dark days following Lilian's death had been brought back to him once more with Cindy's betrayal. There was more than one thing he couldn't work out but he recognised he needed to put all of those thoughts into a box, put a lid on it and get on with his life. He didn't want to waste what was left of it. Having got to grips with this, he now was feeling much better with himself and with the world.

Around the same time as Jonty walked by the river, back in his home town, his old adversary Colin was having to put his house on the market. This had been preceded by the auction of his fleet of top end cars. Nothing was being said other than Colin was having some cashflow difficulties. That was something that was of no surprise to Jonty, he would have been disappointed if it had been otherwise.

Jonty walked to the restaurant and sat down at a table that overlooked the river. He was shaded by an umbrella that nicely took the edge off the midday sun. It was a beautiful day. All around it was a beautiful day. He picked up an ice cold glass of lager that was waiting for him.

"Hello, you three." he commenced, raising his glass to his friends.

Chapter Eleven
Business as Unusual

Dave liked Australia and particularly Melbourne. Australians and their businesses had a freshness that he found invigorating although he didn't feel quite as invigorated when encountering a mob of yahoos on their way to a game of Aussie Rules. A bit like Jonty with his former police mates, what Dave thought was important in business was having good relationships. There is a strain in business that follows the dogma of 'if you can't measure it then you can't manage it.' Dave didn't believe all things were measurable no matter what people thought. Part of being in business was friendships and that was something you couldn't measure and a big part of friendship was humour and camaraderie.

Sometimes, Dave would be involved in business developments which depended on a degree of secrecy for at least their initial impact. When he was in that situation Dave always turned to his team and told them to remember the Oedipus Principle. People who were unfamiliar with this would ask what it was. "Keeping mum," he'd answer.

Dave thought his stoicism might have originated in his experiences when working in his student holidays at an engineering firm. The firm had adapted a farm tractor to use as an indoor mobile crane. This tractor had a short jib on the front and tons of weight strapped on its rear. One day it was tasked with lifting a steel structure that had been fabricated literally on the shop floor. This was a huge ask for such a Heath Robinson piece of machinery. As it slowly started to lift its load people jumped on the rear of the tractor to try and keep its back wheels on the ground. Slowly the load came to an upright position but as it neared the point of being clear of the ground the load lurched from leaning towards the tractor to away from it. The sudden movement broke the chains holding the load which crashed to the ground with an almighty bang and the people holding onto the back of the tractor were catapulted in all directions. Dave wondered if his ears would ever stop ringing. Along with everyone else he stood around and stared at the steelwork. He noticed that caps were taken off before there was much head scratching and head shaking accompanied with the universal one-word language of the day – 'bugger'.

Sadly, mistakes did happen in business. Dave had worked for a motor vehicle assembler at one time. The company was known for being innovative. At one point they were the first to offer a driver's door mirror as a standard fitting on the new model they were bringing to the market. The replacement parts branch of the company decided there was a good opportunity for them. They ordered in a considerable number of passenger door mirrors believing that the people who bought a car with just the driver's mirror on it would want the passenger one as well. Unfortunately, the mirrors were destined to sit on the shelves. After 18 months it was more than obvious these mirrors were not going to sell so they were disposed of at a heavily discounted price. The lesson was learnt.

Three months after that, a considerable number of passenger door mirrors were delivered to the parts warehouse from the manufacturers. When disposing of the old mirrors someone had forgotten to suppress the demand in the computerised parts system, which resulted in the mirrors that were disposed of being automatically re-ordered. A costly mistake which in some environments would have resulted in someone being fired. This company took the view that they knew that person who had made the mistake would never make it again. It wasn't just that person that felt valued but all those surrounding him as well. Dave thought such things weren't truly measurable no matter how many staff surveys you carried out.

Perversely, Dave was aware that loyalty to an organization didn't always pay off. There was a former colleague who had gone to work for a company that had had problems in recent times and some new managers had been introduced to turn it around, Dave's colleague was one of this new team. He knew at the time that Dave wasn't particularly happy where he was and had encouraged him to apply for a new senior role that the organization was looking to fill. Dave was more than keen and at short notice he was asked to attend an interview, the result of which he was one of two who were invited back for further discussions. Dave liked the company and found he got on well with the new Chief Executive, they seemed to have a lot in common. He had a good feeling about it and hoped he was going to be offered the position. He wasn't and was more than disappointed when the job was given to the other candidate.

Dave subsequently moved on as did his former colleague who was offered a role in academia which he felt he couldn't resist. Time went on and occasionally Dave saw some of the great things that that organization was up to. Dave sighed inwardly; he thought it would have been nice to have been a part of it all but recognised that it wasn't to be.

A couple of years later Dave saw the headlines about that Chief Executive being charged with fraud. Dave was flabbergasted, he would never have picked that person as being a fraudster. The person who had blown the whistle on him was the person who had been given the role that Dave had so coveted. The Chief Executive subsequently was found not guilty of fraud although those close to the action maintained that that didn't mean he was innocent. As for the person who blew the whistle on him, he had great difficulty finding another job. Whilst it wasn't overtly said, nobody wanted to employ a whistle blower.

Dave was aware that well-intentioned actions could be misunderstood. In the early years of his marriage, he and his wife had visited his favourite city, York. Unusually, for them they had visited the cafeteria in Woolworths for a coffee and a sandwich. This was in the days when Woolworth's still had department stores in Britain. Nearing the end of his coffee Dave decided he'd visit the toilet. Having achieved what he'd set out to achieve, Dave went to flush it. Sadly, it didn't work. On closer inspection the toilet's cistern had been vandalised. On even closer inspection Dave reckoned he could fix it and so be able to leave the toilet in a clean condition for anybody following him. The fittings thankfully were only finger tight, so Dave soon had the cistern stripped down, the particular offending brass rod straightened out and in no time at all, or so he thought, the cistern was back together and functioning. When he came out, of the cubicle he was surprised to see there was a queue of three or four people who universally gave him a black look whilst muttering away to each other. When he got back to his table his wife told him that she was worried because he'd been in the toilet for so long. After he'd explained what had happened, he was quickly exited from the store and told to leave it to others to fix in the future. Dave really didn't understand what all the fuss was about, he was only trying to be helpful.

Dave knew that being misunderstood could equally apply to relationships where factors beyond your control could come into play and there was little you could do about it. When still a student Dave was given a sports car for his use. His friend was leaving to go to university ahead of Dave. The car had recently been painted but was a non-runner. Dave called on a friend for a favour who called on another friend for a favour. The result was that the car was towed a few miles to be parked outside of Dave's mother's house. The journey had been largely uneventful except that the car arrived looking as if it had contracted a dose of chicken pox en route. Closer inspection revealed that the cars dints and abrasions had been filled with Polyfilla prior to it being painted. This filler isn't renowned for adhering to metal. Consequently, as the car had hit bumps and potholes on its journey across town, bits and pieces of the Polyfilla had broken free leaving it very pock marked. That was the least of Dave's worries, his main concern was that it didn't go.

Dave's mate Jim was a bit of a mechanical wiz. Over the following days he was testing everything he could. After inspecting the body where he discovered some rot in the ash frame he moved onto the wheels and braking system. He didn't think they were too bad, but he'd only know for certain when he got some power into the car and got it rolling. First to get the treatment was the carburetor and fuel pump. They were stripped, scrubbed, scrutinized, blown at, and frowned over. Once everything was put back together it was ascertained that some fuel was flowing, whether the carb. or the jet was set up properly was another matter but at least fuel could get through to the engine. Jim then checked to see if the electrics were alright. After taking a spark plug out and putting it near the engine block, he hoped to see a spark, but there was none. Whilst he contemplated what could be wrong, he thought they should have the head off the engine and polish up the valves. Some weeks later all had been done that could be done. The electrics were still a mystery.

Further examination of the electrics revealed that the Bakelite screw holding in the high-tension lead to the coil was broken. Someone, somewhere, had decided to repair this using a rubbery Bostik adhesive. Great quantities had been used which had congealed into a sticky mass at one of the most crucial points of wanting the best electrical contact that you could possibly get. This was cleaned out and every effort made to establish a good electrical contact. Whether the failing was there or elsewhere a spark was not obtained that day or any other day. Unfortunately, Dave didn't have the money to buy any replacement parts either new or used.

The quest to get the car going again turned from weeks into months. The car had a new battery which Jim borrowed one day because he was having troubles with his own car and promised to return it to Dave's friend when he'd finished with it. After this all efforts to get the car going again faded. Dave had no choice but to call in the scrap merchant to take it away. He was given thirty bob for it which in time he passed on to the friend who'd given the car to him. His friend was surprised it was so little.

His friend's skepticism wasn't helped by a mutual friend of both of theirs who worked for pocket money in the scrapyard where the car had gone. His friend had enquired how much had Dave been given for the car. He was told, quite correctly, that it was in the books as being bought for fifty bob. Sadly, Dave only learnt of this conversation a long time later from their mutual friend and could only assume the scrap merchant was working a tax fiddle. And it wasn't helped by Jim never quite finishing with the battery. But it was too late by then and the damage had been done. Life had moved on and a valued friendship of a number of years had by then become remote. These sorts of things are never measurable.

Chapter Twelve

Love and War

By now Dave found himself almost at Audrey Grove where he'd been nurtured in his early years. Fields he used to roam across and play in as a child were now tarmac and concrete, schools and houses. The allotments where his father grew vegetables for the family had long since gone along with the air raid shelter which had been used as the garden shed. The beck that had run alongside the allotments had disappeared in pipes under the ground and the hawthorn bushes bordering it were no longer there to host May blossoms and the nests of a variety of birds.

The air raid shelter come garden shed had ended up in a neighbour's garden. As a child he couldn't imagine this corrugated iron structure being dug into the small back garden of his house, covered in earth and with concrete poured around it to prevent flooding. Even less could he imagine a couple of families, sometimes more, settling down in it for a night once the air raid sirens had sounded their warning. He was told his mother would stand outside counting the aircraft taking off from the local airbase and count them back in the morning, the arithmetic of tragedy.

War, when spoken about, was the time of a close camaraderie whether on the home front or on the battle field. The only dissenting voice was against the spivs, the black marketeers and stupid officers and officials who made men and women do unnecessary things. In the middle of a hurly burly active front to be called to parade to practise saluting was considered not only unnecessary, but bordering on the criminal. To the winners, they won in spite of such idiots, and what they wanted was a fairer world after all their sacrifices and a better place for their children.

The war was a time when love had to endure long separations, uncertain communications, and the worry of not knowing. The winners were never sure if there really were any winners in war and the casualties continued to grow long after peace was declared and were largely uncounted. Dave had heard of more than one love story set against these fraught times.

Gabrielle hadn't meant to fall in love, if anything, she'd been warned against it. She lived in a small market town with a river running through the middle of it. It didn't have a lot of historical buildings remaining, no cute castle or half-timbered dwellings, leastwise genuine ones, but plenty of 19th century charm. Apart from being the centre for farmlands and woods that surrounded it, the town had developed its own industry, largely engineering but was known for its timber and woodworking as well. Thankfully, none of this impinged too badly on the charms of the town, the worst bits were comfortably hidden away, down wind.

Gabrielle, for the want of something to do, had gone window shopping one fine day in early spring. Why she bothered she wasn't quite sure but it made her feel alive. She knew it was wartime, she knew there wasn't much to see through the brown sticky tape criss-crossed windows and that, which wasn't a cardboard replica or a faded poster, was either unattainable or unaffordable. Notwithstanding, all the anxieties and uncertainties that war had brought to the town's doorstep, for this one moment, she couldn't and didn't want to suppress the light headiness she felt. After such a dreadfully cold and bitter winter maybe it was the warmth she could now feel in the air, maybe it was that gentle breeze that brushed her skin and invigorated. There was a lightness in her soul and she was delighted to be alive.

Gabrielle lived in a small cottage on the edge of the town. It was up a path from the road that ran by the river. It had been her grandmother's home and she had inherited it when she was 18 years old. She'd lived with her grandmother after her parents had died; killed when an out of control bus had run into them. At times, when she was alone by herself in the cottage, the melancholy of her losses would overwhelm her happy disposition and ready smile. That sadness and those memories were hers and hers alone; they were not for sharing. Once she was through the front door, going out and about, she found a brisk talking to herself and a quick nip on the back of her hand made sure her privacy remained behind those closed doors.

It was his reflection she first noticed as she looked into a forlorn shop window. He looked smart in his uniform but what really attracted her first was his face. Well not so much his face as his smile. The war had seen soldiers billeted into a country house on the other side of town away from where she lived. All the young men and not so young men had all been taken away from the town to serve their country in one form or another, even some of the not so able bodied and lead swingers had all gone. In their place were the soldiers in the country house. All had been quietly warned to stay away from these soldiers, especially the young women, who were told to steer clear. The older women whose sons and husbands had been taken from them were particularly vociferous. The soldiers had coin in their pocket and weren't to be trusted. Leave well alone.

Gabrielle couldn't have told you how they started talking, all she knew was that she wouldn't have made the first move. His voice was as sweet as his smile, there was a genuineness about him. He was easy going and not pushy. As she walked along he began to walk alongside her. They talked about this and that but not much about themselves or the war, certainly not about the war, why spoil such a lovely day. They smiled a lot at each other.

After a while Gabrielle thanked Ralph for his company but told him she was going home. Ralph asked if he could walk her home. She politely declined. He persisted and said he'd like to see her again, could they meet again next week? She agreed, and they fixed to meet the following week by the Stone Bridge.

Gabrielle worked at a small timber mill; it was a five and a half day week. It was now run by older men and women with most of the product being commandeered for the war effort. Everyone would have preferred the wood to have gone into making and repairing houses and making other useful things but they had no choice. It was a friendly team. Early resentment by the men of women doing men's jobs gave way to acceptance and grudging admiration. Early attempts at placing uninvited hands on a woman's backside as they leaned forward in their overalls undertaking their tasks, were soon curtailed by a swift tap around the ankles with the sweeping up broom.

Cries of "there's no need for that" by the men, were met with the response,

"Well, you know what not to do if you don't want it to happen again."

Gabrielle's week passed by quickly, she was surprised as to how much she was looking forward to seeing Ralph on Sunday. She told herself not to be stupid and anyway she thought he might not turn up. Despite her reservations she knew she was going to be disappointed if he wasn't there.

When Sunday came around Gabrielle made a bit more of an effort than usual when getting ready although she told herself she wasn't really. She didn't want to appear over eager so left home with the aim of being five minutes late. Long enough to make him wait but short enough so that he didn't give up and walk away. She arrived at the bridge but could see no sign of him. Maybe he'd misunderstood where they were going to meet and had gone to the other end. Because of the arch in the bridge you couldn't see one end of the bridge from the other. After looking around and seeing no sign of Ralph, Gabrielle set to walk to the other end. She walked to the apex and a little more just to make sure she could clearly see but there was no one there. "Soldiers!" she thought to herself, "It must be true what everyone says."

She turned around to walk home with a stomp in her step. She reached the end of the bridge where they were supposed to meet and turned for home. She hadn't gone fifty yards when she heard her name being called. She turned around to find Ralph running for all he was worth after her. When he caught up he apologised profusely.

"I'm so very sorry," he breathlessly spluttered, "the sergeant had me do extra sentry duties this morning when I was supposed to be off duty. I thought I was never going to get away."

Gabrielle quickly forgave him and they decided to go for a walk by the river. There were some steps built into a wall that had to be negotiated before you could join the path. Ralph took Gabrielle's hand to guide her over and then didn't leave go. Gabrielle didn't object. The river had sufficient water in it to make it babble along with an intoxicating liveliness about it. The greens of the trees had that fresh bright greenness you see in spring. Life was for living.

Ralph told Gabrielle about himself. He had served an apprenticeship as a cabinet maker, he enjoyed working with wood, he had great satisfaction out of not only making things but creating things as well. His parents were dead, his father had been gassed in the last war and had died prematurely due to the damage to his lungs. His mother had taken the loss badly and had slowly pined away once she thought Ralph could stand on his own two feet. He had lived in a bedsit near to where he worked but with being conscripted into the army he had now lost that so technically he was of no fixed abode. He was pleased to have been assigned to the medical corps, he was also pleased that most of the time he didn't have to carry a rifle, he thought wars were stupid but in the current environment it was even stupider to express such a thought. Gabrielle stroked his forearm as he told her about himself. She thanked him for doing so but to lighten the mood a little she picked up on one point with a smile on her face.

"So are you truly of no fixed abode?"

"Truly, of no fixed abode. The few things I have are in cases in a warehouse."

"Therefore, it's true to say that you are a tramp?"

"I suppose you're right. I'll have to buy a Charlie Chaplin

hat." From that day forward Gabrielle would refer to Ralph at intimate times as Tramp, but always with a smile.

Gabrielle told Ralph about herself. He stopped walking, gave her a hug and then kissed her. From that point they became more and more inseparable. They didn't advertise that they were a couple and met and walked as much as possible away from other people. Gabrielle knew that some people, if they knew, would regard her as a tart for going out with a soldier. She preferred to avoid the confrontation. Ralph was equally aware that some people would think ill of Gabrielle and wanted to protect her as much as he could.

They enjoyed each other's company, they found so much in common, their approach to life, their humour, they were always making fun of each other and more than anything else they found themselves in love. They talked of marriage once this war was over and Ralph could return to cabinet making. To be married, Ralph knew he needed the Army's permission and in those times that was never going to be given.

The only person Gabrielle fully confided in was her long-time friend Caroline. She'd been friends with Caroline since schooldays, they'd shared all their secrets. She was Caroline's bridesmaid when she'd married Hugo and godmother when they had baby Leo. Caroline was happy for Gabrielle but was worried for her. She knew there were some who would resent her going out with a soldier and as soldiers weren't allowed out of camp other than in uniform it was difficult to keep the romance totally secret. Gabrielle and Ralph visited Caroline and Hugo from time to time, when they would sit around the table playing card or board games.

Spring turned to summer, summer to autumn and autumn to winter. The romance flourished and any objections were whispered. When winter started, baby Leo became unwell and during January his condition worsened, he became dangerously ill. The doctor said he needed a medicine that was impossible to obtain in those times. When Ralph heard about this he asked what it was that was wanted. He was able to obtain some from the army stores and so Leo was treated and was soon back to being a healthy toddler. Caroline and Hugo couldn't have been more grateful.

Louis was a middle aged man who managed one of the town's engineering companies. He'd cosied up to the military and all of the company's output was directed to what the army wanted. He often visited the army camp as part of his business. He was a chancer, if there was money to be made he'd be there wanting a piece of the action. He loudly sang his own praises and was ready to blame others when things didn't go his way, nothing was ever his fault. Some people wondered how he'd managed to be able to stay in the town when so many of the other men had been conscripted and sent away.

Caroline hadn't meant to compromise Ralph but when people asked about Leo she must have been unable to hide her gratitude to him. Louis had heard whispers and it wasn't long before he was knocking on Caroline's door. He said he'd heard Ralph had helped her when her baby was ill. Did she think he would help him as his wife was in a bad way. Caroline said that she would ask next time she saw him. Louis said there was some urgency. Caroline agreed to contact Gabrielle to get a message to Ralph. Louis gave her a note with the names of the medicines that he needed.

When Ralph received the request he said he'd see what he could do. He told Caroline and Gabrielle to be cautious around Louis and don't trust him as he tittle-tattled about people at the Army base.

Ralph was able to get the medicines for Louis and decided

to deliver them directly to his home. He wasn't invited in and handed over the medicines on the door step. He was profusely thanked but in whispered tones. As he walked away from the house he looked back and saw a woman bustling about in one of the rooms. If that was Louis's wife then Ralph had suspicions about how ill she really was.

In some ways it came as no surprise to Ralph that a few days later, as he headed to see Gabrielle, that he was approached by Louis. Louis thanked him for the medicines and asked him if it was possible to get anymore. Ralph asked if the medicines had helped Louis's wife at all.

"Yeah, yeah, yeah," replied Louis quickly and dismissively. "If you can get me more like that then I can sell them. There'll be something in it for you. It'll be worth your while."

"I don't do that sort of thing," replied Ralph very icily. Louis persisted but saw he was getting nowhere. His anger increased when he received yet another rebuff.

"You'll regret it," said Louis before walking away in a huff.

It wasn't long after this that Ralph warned Gabrielle that all the signs were pointing to him being posted. There were apparently a lot of meetings behind closed doors and scurrying about by the senior officers. He told Gabrielle that he may not be able to let her know when or where he was going. He told her how much he loved her and said that God willing, he would return. Gabrielle told Ralph she loved him and would wait for him to come back. She begged him to come back safely.

Then one day Ralph was no longer there. The Army base was locked down for 48 hours with no one allowed in or out and then they were gone.

∞

It was a good four years after the war had ended when there was a knock on Hugo and Caroline's door. It was Caroline who opened it. A man stood there saying nothing.

"Yes?" she said, "Can I help you?"

"I'm Ralph, do you remember me?" Caroline looked again and then recognised him. He had aged more than the 5 years since she had last seen him.

"Come in, do come in." Ralph walked rather tiredly in. Without asking, Caroline went to make a hot drink and bring out some homemade cake whilst Hugo made him comfortable.

"You look tired," said Hugo.

"Yes, it's been a long journey back here." It looked like Ralph was going to say something else but Caroline had come bustling in with cake and drinks. After Ralph had sipped his drink, he toyed with his cake while looking at his feet

"I went up to Gabrielle's cottage but all I found was an overgrown burnt out ruin. Can you tell me where I can find her, please?" Hugo and Caroline looked at each other before Hugo spoke, he knew Caroline would be unable to.

"I'm sorry," said Hugo. Ralph hung his head and tears silently ran down his nose.

"Did she get tired of waiting for me?"

"I'm sorry," Hugo repeated himself, "sadly she died."

"What happened?" asked Ralph after a pause.

"After you and all the other soldiers left and the war heated up," started Hugo, "life became chaotic around here. Vigilante groups sprang up, some allegedly righting wrongs and bringing justice to the town, some were just settling old scores and some were outright gangsters. Because of Gabrielle's relationship with you, she was at risk. You may remember Louis, he said he'd look after her. The price for his protection was that she was to become his mistress."

"What a sordid little man!" burst out Ralph. "I'm sure he was behind me being separated from my mates and sent to another front where I ended up being taken a prisoner of war. All because I wouldn't supply him with medicines to sell. A horrid little man!"

"Anyway, I suppose you'd know that Gabrielle told him where he could go. She told us about his approach. We were worried for her and urged her to leave town and go and live somewhere else. She wouldn't. She said that you were returning for her and if she wasn't there then you wouldn't know where to find her. We pleaded with her to go and said we'd keep a look out for you but she was stubborn. She wanted to be in the cottage for you when you returned." Hugo was silent for a while whilst Ralph's silent tears continued to run down his nose and Caroline wiped her eyes with a handkerchief.

"One night the vigilantes struck and burnt Gabrielle's cottage. Her charred body was later found inside. Most people thought that Louis lay behind the attack and that he'd gone too far."

"Was Louis made to pay for what he did?" asked Ralph.

"I'm afraid not. Nothing sticks to Louis. He's now our mayor."

"Proof, I suppose, that it's not only cream that floats," said Ralph rather bitterly. After a pause he continued rather wearily,

"Oh why did she wait for me?"

"Because she loved you," said Hugo.

"Love, I think was only ever going to be allowed for the winners of this war. For the losers it could only ever be a tragedy. For a German soldier like me, I was never going to be allowed to live happily ever after with my own very dear French mademoiselle."

Chapter Thirteen
The Dilemma

Dave was starting to make his way back to his hotel. He thought he'd walked sufficiently around the town and around his memories. He was feeling exhausted but not quite sure whether it was physical, mental or both. All this meant that he was going to savour a nice glass of red wine when he finally put his feet up for the day. He knew he wouldn't find one of his favourite New Zealand or Australian wines but was not averse to a good drop from France, or Italy, or for that matter a good Spanish wine. The very idea was banishing his weariness as he walked along.

His thoughts digressed as he passed an opticians. He recalled a woman who had had an operation for the cataracts on her eyes. Not long after, she visited her doctor to express her concern at the side effects she was suffering from. The doctor was somewhat surprised as he said it was unusual to have side effects from that procedure but not entirely unknown. Before conferring with the specialist who'd conducted the operation the doctor needed to know the exact details of her side effects.

"Isn't it obvious, can't you see?" asked the woman. "As soon as I looked in the mirror I noticed. Look at all these wrinkles around my eyes."

Dave's silent reverie at this nonsensical recollection was interrupted by someone calling to him using an old nickname he hadn't heard for years.

"Hey, Longpockets, is that you?"

"Goodness gracious me Crud, what a sight for sore eyes."

"A pint in the Boot and Shoe?" asked Crud. Dave nodded his acceptance and they turned and headed towards a hostelry that seemed to have been there since time immemorial. Crud recalled going out with a daughter of the licensee many years ago. He'd lost track of her when she'd gone to London to pursue her dancing career.

After they'd settled down at a table with their drinks they rediscovered their actual names, Sean said it was the first time he'd been called Crud in many a long year. Dave equally admitted that his nickname seemed to be something from a long and distant past. He acknowledged that he may well have been awarded other nicknames during his career but they weren't necessarily something that were shared with him.

After Sean had enquired, Dave gave him a potted history of his family and life in New Zealand. He told Sean he was on a bit of a nostalgia binge. After he'd finished he asked,

"And what of you Sean? What are you doing back here?"

"I was down in the South-West working in the aircraft industry. I was there for a few years suffering being made redundant more than once when the orders dried up. I was also 'restructured' when someone came along who thought they knew better than I did. Sometimes, I came back here to lick my wounds and sometimes not. The last redundancy paid me out generously and I felt too old to be faced with another round of 'on again, off again' so, I've returned back home to stay. I've picked up a canny little job with the pensions' people here. It pays alright and I've none of the stresses and strains I had before. I'm happy."

"Have you any family, wife and kids?" asked Dave.

"No, I can't say I've been overly lucky in love. I've been married more than once and had a couple of live ins but all water under the bridge at the end of the day."

"Anybody at the moment?" enquired Dave.

"Well, yes and yes," replied Sean.

"Yes and yes?" repeated Dave with his face expressing the question mark.

"Let me explain," started Sean. "A little while ago I was invited to a charity auction in a pub. I wasn't overly keen on going and it wasn't the best of nights weatherwise but I went as it was for Save the Children. I ended up sitting at a table with some people I didn't particularly know but joined in the fun as best as I was able. The small chat was polite but on the strained side. There was a couple of big noters there bidding away trying to impress the crowd with their flamboyant generosity but largely succeeding in getting up everyone's noses. I was looking forward to escaping at the first opportunity. It seemed a bit rude to disappear too early so, as I was by myself, I headed to the bar to buy myself a drink as much for something to do as opposed to particularly wanting a drink. I'd just ordered a glass of wine when a woman snook in beside me at the bar and ordered champagne from another barman. The barman told her they didn't sell champagne by the glass.

'That's fine,' she replied, 'a bottle will do, Moet if you have it.'

'How many glasses?' asked the barman.

'One, thank you,' the woman replied. As you may imagine this made me look and there beside me was this gorgeous woman maybe a couple of years younger than me.

'Celebrating by yourself?' I enquired.

'No, but if I'm going to have a glass of wine I much prefer it to have a touch of quality about it particularly when I'm here with more a sense of duty rather than enthusiasm. Goodness, I hope those plonkers cough up what they have bid at the end of the night!'

'I know how you feel and can't disagree with you.' I responded. That introduction quickly started a delightful conversation; it was as if we were long lost friends. As the room was called to order to resume the auction, Odette, for that was her name, invited me to join her table as there was a spare seat. I willingly agreed knowing full well I wouldn't be missed at the table where I'd been sitting.

It turned out that Odette was divorced, with a couple of grown up children who had fled the coup. In no time at all I was dating her and not long after that I was staying over. It was and is a wonderful feeling something which I hadn't experienced through my marriages and other liaisons, above all else it was fun. I hadn't smiled so much for many a long year. I couldn't ask for more. I could see myself heading in front of a marriage celebrant again but with no sense of foreboding."

"Congratulations, I'm really pleased for you," said Dave,

"you deserve it."

"Thanks," said Sean "that's kind of you." Sean paused, dropped his head a little and looked pensive.

"Is there something wrong?" asked Dave.

"A couple of days ago I went for a walk by the Bishop's Palace in Bishop Auckland, I went down to the River Gauntless, just past the deer house. I don't know what took me there as I hadn't been there for years. As I was walking back I heard my name being called. It was Pru. You may remember her; I had an affair with her years ago and I thought she was going to leave her husband and go off with me and we were going to get married. So much for what thought did. Anyway she stayed with her husband and I went off to my first marriage disaster. A few years later I happened to be back in Darlo and heard her husband had died. I thought I'd look her up and hopefully we'd take up where we left off. Again you know what thought did. She left me in no uncertain terms she didn't want me in her life. Once again I left town with my tail between my legs."

"Was it too soon after her husband's death?" asked Dave.

"It could have been," said Sean, "or it could have been that I may well have been the father of her son."

"Wow! Really?"

"Put it this way, I looked an awful lot like him at his age."

"You didn't pursue it any further?" asked Dave.

"No, what was the point?"

"Sorry, I'm digressing. You said you'd seen Pru again," encouraged Dave.

"As I said, there she was calling my name. Notwithstanding what had gone on before I was delighted to see her and told her so. She said she'd often thought about me and was pleased to see me.

'Really', I said, 'I would have thought after our last meeting you were more pleased to see the back of me.'

'I was thinking about my son, Bob. I didn't want him to get hurt. I'm sorry, I was such a bitch.' Pru said. I asked her how Bob was these days.

'Bob's fine, he's part of a new IT start up in Cambridge. He's loving it. When he was older I told him about our affair and the possibility that Ken may not be his biological father. He told me that Ken was his father and the only one he wanted. He had no curiosity about you and no particular desire to want to meet with you but said he wouldn't go out of his way to avoid you either. Sorry Sean.'

I told her I was happy that he was happy. I asked about her business that she was running when I last saw her. She told me that it had gone from strength to strength. She'd moved into offices and a yard in Northallerton when she could no longer manage from home, they'd also opened yards in Whitby, York and Hull. They had a good reputation and the work kept coming in. When Slim, her right hand man, had decided to retire she'd asked Bob if he was interested in joining the firm. She said she knew the answer but he had to be given the chance and wasn't surprised or disappointed that he wanted to stay in the IT world. So, she said she sold the business to another company they had worked with over the years and with whom they got on well. She knew the company would continue to flourish and more importantly that the personnel who worked there would be fairly treated. She said she moved back to Darlo from the North Yorkshire Moors. She told me it had been lovely living there but you couldn't get away from fact that the winters could be bleak and anyway she could afford a hotel on the moors in the summer if that's what took her fancy." After taking time to savour his drink, Sean continued,

"Anyway, before we knew it we were chatting away and

laughing and smiling like old times. It was just so lovely and my heart was stirring for her all over again. We're meeting up tomorrow to go for a walk along the river to High Force."

"What about Odette?" asked Dave.

"I don't know, I really don't know. Women! They're like buses, you don't see one for ages and ages and then two turn up at once."

THE END

Made in the USA
Monee, IL
06 October 2022

15178526R00075